Bringing Vincent Home

a novel

by Madeleine Mysko

Plain View Press
P. O. 42255
Austin, TX 78704

plainviewpress.net
sb@plainviewpress.net
1-512-441-2452

ISBN: 978-1-891386-78-7
Library of Congress Number: 9781891386787

Cover painting: *The Wall*, by Aurence; private collection of Dr. Kathy Bates.

In memory of the wounded who died, and in honor of those who survived.

And in memory of my father, Thomas Vincent Seipp, a sailor at the age of seventeen, who kept his own war stories locked in his heart.

Acknowledgements

I acknowledge and thank the Maryland State Arts Council for the generous Individual Artist grant in support of this novel, and the Sewanee Writers Conference for the encouragement implied in the scholarships granted to me.

I am grateful to the late Dr. Andrew M. Munster for the expertise — both medical and literary — he lent to this novel at its earliest stage.

I thank my mentors and readers: Jessica Blau, Joshua Brown, Meg Waite Clayton, the late Al Cyford, Lindsay Fleming, Eric Freeman, Anne Frydman, Jo Krause, Alice McDermott, Claire Mysko, Martha Mysko, Gene Oishi, Sabine Oishi, Heather O'Brien, Arthur Rogers, Phyllis Rogers, John Sasser, Tracy Wallace, Thomas Woolfolk, and my husband, John Sheehan.

For years of creative sustenance, I also thank the poets: Joyce Stevens Brown, Ann LoLordo, Kathleen O'Toole, Natasha Sajé, and especially Christine Higgins, who carefully ushered this novel toward the light.

I know that I am blessed: My mother gave birth to the storyteller in me, and my own children — Claire, Joseph, Luke, and Martha — have nurtured that storyteller since they were very young.

Prologue

Last year a photograph of me — along with two other women from the Calvert Park Apartments — appeared on the front page of *The Baltimore Sun*. I'm the one in the big hat, holding the sign with the number of soldiers killed in Iraq.

We're out there every Friday between noon and one, unless bad weather forbids. I usually wear an over-sized black T-shirt with a white peace symbol on the front. If it's cold, I wear my good black coat.

It's a great photograph, and after it appeared I got phone calls from people I hadn't seen in ages, including Alma Henderson, who lived next door to me forty years ago in the old neighborhood. Alma is ninety-two now. The first thing she said to me was, "Are you crazy, hon?" and we had a good laugh.

I put the clipping from*The Sun* on the shelf in my dining area, next to the old photograph of me with my son Vincent, which was taken in December 1968, on the Sunday before he left for Vietnam. In that photograph, we're standing in front of the house on Constance Avenue. Vincent is wearing his uniform, and he's smiling right into the camera. Of course I'm smiling too, though perhaps less confidently.

In truth, all these years I have never been one to take part in peace demonstrations. And so the irony in a newspaper clipping of me — an old woman now, sitting out there on a beach chair with a peace symbol on my shirt — wasn't lost on my daughter Mary Kate. "Look at you, Mom," she said, with a sly smile.

I like it that on Fridays this group of women sits silently at the curb, dressed in black and holding up calls for peace to the cars passing by. But week after week, as I held the number of the dead on my lap, something was gnawing at me: Was it enough?

One day I sat down at the computer the children gave me for Christmas and began to write for all I was worth. My name is Kitty Duvall. I'm eighty-four now, and I know my memory isn't perfect. But in the writing I lived it all over again.

1

It was late afternoon, and I'd just dropped the last piece of chicken into the skillet, when the phone rang. I assumed it was my mother, who often called around that time of day, right after the soaps.

But it was not my mother. It was an official, military voice informing me that Vincent had been injured and that they'd be flying him from Vietnam to Japan, and from Japan to the burn ward in Texas. I was so upset, my hands still covered in flour, that I scribbled the words on the bottom of the calendar next to the phone: *Japan, Brooke Army Medical Center, burn ward* — terrible words in blue ink, under the picture for August, 1969, a picture of three German shepherd puppies in a basket.

And I remember staring at the flame under the old black skillet, thinking about the pain of just one little spit of grease on the forearm. I had no idea where Vincent had been burned — his arms, his hands, his face? I only knew I had to get to wherever he was, and see for myself.

It was three days before I could fly to Texas, and when I got there it was as though I'd been yanked from the life I'd always known and dropped onto a blinding hot tarmac. The air of San Antonio felt suffocating and strange — the air of someone else's life, not mine. Everywhere I looked there were people in uniform, reminding me oddly of Penn Station in Baltimore during the forties, those years that members of my generation will always refer to as "The War," as if there were no other.

I managed to claim my old brown leather suitcase, which I'd had to root out of the attic the day before. Sitting there among the other people's bags, it looked only vaguely familiar, like something worrisome floating up in a bad dream. At the "Military Reception" desk, I asked about Fort Sam Houston, but the young man there informed me politely that his services were for active duty personnel.

From behind me came a hearty voice: "You're headed for Fort Sam, ma'am?"

I turned to see a tall man in an old-fashioned fedora, the brim dipping over his brow like a gangster's hat in the movies. In the shadow of that brim I could see his red-rimmed, watery-blue eyes, and his awful pinched nose. He was smiling — I knew this, even though the scars on his neck had pulled the chin and mouth downward in the wrong direction. And I knew he was young, despite his conservative khaki chinos and white dress shirt.

I answered yes — I was going to Fort Sam Houston, to Brooke Army Medical Center.

"Allow me," he said, and I was startled to see his hand — so scarred — grab my suitcase and swing it forward. "Let's get you a cab."

He moved fast, and I had to trot to keep up.

"I'm guessing you're here to visit your son," he said over his shoulder.

"Right. Are you heading that way too?"

He gave a short, pleasant laugh. "No ma'am, but I've put in my time there, believe me."

"So you're in the Army?"

"Not any more."

He led me to the line of cabs along the curb, and immediately a driver in a cowboy hat sprang forward to take my suitcase.

It all happened so fast. When the cab pulled away, I looked over my shoulder. The kind young man with the ruined face — the burned young man — had disappeared already. I was distressed I hadn't asked his name, not knowing then that we would meet again.

2

Of the three children, why was Vincent always the one with the problem? The older two, Mary Kate and Jack, just breezed along, never giving the nuns at St. Anthony's a moment's trouble, always bringing home good report cards, and finally getting scholarships to college. But Vincent struggled from the day I handed him over, bawling and digging in his heels at the door to Sister Therese's first grade classroom.

I tried to keep after him, checking his homework each night, having Mary Kate sit with him at the dining room table to do the spelling and study for the tests. But Vincent was forever losing papers or leaving books in his desk at school. The nuns would send notes home, and I'd find them crumpled up in his book-bag or among the crumbs in his lunchbox. "Dear Mrs. Duvall," and always something about Vincent not progressing satisfactorily. The nuns thought Vincent just needed a firm hand. They were aware — though of course they never mentioned it — that my husband Frank was pretty much out of the picture by the time Vincent was in third grade.

When Vincent got to high school, I guess I hoped that Jack, who was a junior when Vincent was a freshman, might keep his little brother in line. But by then Jack had been cast as the goody-goody, and Vincent just laughed and ran off with the fast crowd. Vincent got suspended for drinking on the parking lot after a mixer. He got kicked off the basketball team for carrying beer onto the bus, and that was the end of his chance for an athletic scholarship to Mount St. Mary's College, which had once seemed so sure. After graduation, he took a job in the Rexall drugstore. He played ball at the recreation center. He bought a guitar, a beat-up old thing he found in the Goodwill Store. He said he didn't want to go to college anyway. He said he wasn't scared of Vietnam.

The months went by, and I kept telling myself that things could turn out all right, if only Mary Kate could take him in hand, if only Jack could. But of course it was the Army that took him in hand, swiftly, before he'd learned more than a couple of chords on that beat-up guitar.

❍

The first thing I noticed about Fort Sam Houston — after the military policeman waved the taxi through the wrought-iron gate — was that wide blue sky above all those red tile roofs. The buildings were mostly yellow, the color of butter.

On the ride from the airport, the taxi driver had made small talk, but I'd been too preoccupied to give more than short answers. Now he looked at me in the rearview mirror and asked me point blank. "So, was your son wounded in action?"

"Yes." *Wounded* seemed like a foreign word, a word I couldn't remember having spoken in my entire life.

"I'm sorry to hear that," he said. "My nephew Carlos — my sister's boy — is over there right now. He's a Warrant Officer, a helicopter pilot, probably flying around as we speak."

I'm sorry to hear that. I kept my eyes on those yellow buildings, the larger ones with their old-fashioned porches running across both upstairs and down. All of them had names printed across the screen doors — captains, majors, colonels, and two generals — and then came the officers' club and then more houses, the same butter color, the same tile roofs. The lawns were well tended, with flower gardens and large palm trees. On one of them, I saw a sign: *Yard of the Month.* I hadn't expected an Army post to look so southern and romantic.

"You got other kids?" the driver asked.

"Two."

Under different circumstances I would have told him about Mary Kate, graduated from college already and out on her own, and Jack, a senior at Loyola, in pre-med. But it made my heart sink to even think about them, far away now in Baltimore, to think about the drive to the airport — Jack at the wheel and Mary Kate turning around from the front seat to add something else to the list of things I ought to find out right away from whoever was in charge of Vincent. When they kissed me goodbye, both of them were crying, though Jack tried to hide it of course.

Fort Sam Houston was a huge compound. There was a long, broad field at its center, baking in the afternoon sun. Along the edge of that field, but out in the road, I saw a platoon of recruits marching along. As the taxi passed, I could hear them singing in response to the drill sergeant: *Box me up and send me home. Sound off . . . One two . . .* Oddly, the call and response put me in mind of the rosary that my mother would listen to every night on the radio at home in Baltimore

— *Hail Mary*, the priest intoning, and *Holy Mary*, the old ladies in the pews answering.

I stared at those boys, at the backs of their shaved heads shining in the sun. No doubt they'd be going to Vietnam, and probably their mothers would press a crease into their uniform trousers, early on the morning of the last day at home, as I had done. I'd been in such a state that day. The whole morning I'd been troubled by the sense that there was something important I ought to have done, and time was getting away from us. When Vincent called from downstairs — *Mom?* — I got distracted and burned myself on the iron. I still have a scar above my left wrist, about the size of a darning needle.

As for Vincent, he had seemed almost happy, geared up for adventure, a soldier with basic training behind him. *Sound off . . . One two . . .* Vincent heading off to war, like it was nothing but a jaunt up the road for a hamburger and a shake.

"That's Brooke Army Medical Center up ahead, ma'am," the driver said.

I looked and saw what appeared to be a brown apparition at the far end of the field. When we got closer, I realized the medical center wasn't the shiny, modern building I'd expected, but an old place with ornate pillars at the entrance and those same red tiles on the roof. Tucked alongside were smaller, matching buildings, like servants' quarters to the mansion. Brooke Army Medical Center was old, but commanding too, with wings rising toward the tower at the center.

The driver pulled up to the curb directly in front and got out to take my suitcase from the trunk.

"Good luck," he said, when I handed him the fare, "to you and your son."

"And to you and your nephew Carlos," I said.

All sorts of military people were passing by — Army greens, Navy blues, khakis and medical-looking whites. Some of them nodded to me, polite but serious, as though they knew exactly why I had come.

Going up the steps, I noticed the pigeons nesting on top of the pillars, above the Latin motto with the huge medical symbol in the middle. *Non sibi sed proximo . . . Not something, but something.* It seemed important to know what it said, but I'd forgotten nearly everything I'd learned in high school, in Sister Mary Anthony's Latin class.

The lobby was cool and dim, with a high ceiling and carved moldings. The soldier at the desk advised me to leave the suitcase with him, and take the elevator. "Fourth floor, ma'am," he said. "Ward 14A. Ask for Colonel Anderson."

The minute I stepped off the elevator, a tall woman in a starched white uniform arrived soundlessly from around the corner. She looked to be in her late forties, though her hair, cut short about her face, was pure white.

"Mrs. Duvall?" she said warmly, and shook my hand right away.

"Yes," I said. "Kitty Duvall. How do you do."

She introduced herself as Colonel Anderson, Chief Nurse. She asked me about the flight from Baltimore.

"Fine, thank you." I tried to be as determinedly cheerful as she was.

She led me down a narrow, cluttered corridor, past a line of stretchers and big wooden wheelchairs, past a strange bed with a big-faced scale attached to it. It was as though I'd stepped backward in time, or into one of those suffocating dreams in which the ceiling keeps getting lower, and the passages tighter. There was a seriously medicinal smell to the place, and under that another smell I didn't recognize, and couldn't bear to think about.

At the first door the Colonel stopped and explained that Vincent's doctor — "Major Caruso, but you can call him Doctor Caruso if you like" — was in surgery, but would come up to the ward as soon as he could. "This won't be easy," she said, holding the door open. "But I'll be here to help."

We washed our hands at a little sink in what looked like a linen closet. She gave me a long surgical gown to put on over my clothes, tied it in back for me, and patted me on the shoulder. I had the feeling I was being prepared for the worst. Then she put a gown on too, over her uniform, and led the way out of the closet.

We came to a small workstation where the nurses and corpsmen were going in and out. They were dressed in surgical suits or gowns, their pockets jammed with scissors and clamps, masks hanging from their necks or tied over their faces. One carried a tray of syringes. Another pushed a cart loaded with bottles and stainless steel pans. Everything about their movements seemed efficient and sure. A young corpsman was swabbing the linoleum floor. I could see that the place was certainly clean — immaculate — and yet for such an important place, the place to which Vincent had been flown immediately, it seemed old, worn, and much too small. In fact, it appeared there wasn't much more to the burn ward than three cramped rooms.

"This is our intensive care unit," Colonel Anderson said, nodding at the room across from the nurses' station. "Better known as the Cube — for cubicle. Your son is out on the ward."

I glanced in at the knot of intravenous lines and machines. I heard the cold, mechanical whooshing of the respirators, and instinctively held my breath.

A skinny nurse with red-blond hair came out of the Cube. Colonel Anderson introduced her as Lieutenant Bukowsky. She didn't look old enough to be a nurse, let alone a lieutenant. Her scrub dress hung nearly to the top of her shoes, even though she'd cinched it and bloused it at the waist. When she hurried away, the extra scrub dress bunched up in the back had the effect of a Victorian bustle.

We came to a ward of eight beds, which opened into another ward of eight. Everything seemed too bright: heat lamps, shining intravenous bottles, the white sheets draped on frames over the beds — over the patients — like tents. Some of the patients were sitting up in chairs, their arms and legs and faces smeared with a white salve or wrapped in dressings. The patient closest to the doorway was propped up in bed, reading a comic book. He seemed even younger to me than my Vincent. I saw he had lost his leg below the knee, and I quickly averted my eyes.

"Hi, Colonel Anderson," the boy said, waving his comic book.

"Hello there, Jimmy."

And then there was Vincent. He was lying beneath his own sheets, which were draped over a circular frame, like an igloo. He slowly turned his head to look at me.

"Hi Mom," he said, and for just a moment I actually thought we'd been spared, because his face hadn't been burned at all. Only the right side of his neck was covered with the thick white salve. He smiled — that crooked smile that said there'd been some sort of trouble, like the time I had to go to the principal's office to bail him out when he got caught smoking in the bathroom.

"Hello, Vinnie." I touched the sheet draped over the frame. It was stiff, still creased from the laundry. I could only wonder what damage was hidden underneath. "Is this any way to get a ride back home?"

Vincent didn't laugh. He was looking past me now, at someone just arriving at the bedside.

"Well here he is," Colonel Anderson said. "Mrs. Duvall, this is Dr. Caruso."

Dr. Caruso's smile was hesitant, or perhaps only weary. He was young, and didn't look particularly military. He needed a shave. The collar of his uniform shirt was poking sloppily from his untied gown. I wondered if he might be right out of training.

Dr. Caruso spoke to Vincent first. "Have we got the pain under control?"

"Yes, sir."

"I'm going to take your mom up to my office for awhile," the doctor said.

"I'll be right back, Sweetheart," I said, but Vincent had already closed his eyes, and didn't answer me.

Colonel Anderson gave me another motherly pat, and returned to the nurses' station. Dr. Caruso led the way, past an area that might have been a sun porch at one time but was cluttered with all sorts of equipment, and into a small office. There was one window, and I could see that outside the sun was still shining fiercely, as though it had gotten stuck at one point in the afternoon. Such a long day — but then I remembered I'd flown into a different time zone, and would have to set my watch.

Dr. Caruso leaned forward with his arms on his knees when he spoke to me. "Mrs. Duvall," he said, "your son has been burned over thirty-six per cent of his body."

Thirty-six per cent.

He explained that each arm counted for nine per cent. Add the area of the chest and neck, and you got another eighteen. The white salve I'd seen on his neck was called Sulfamylon, and was the very best they had for burns. No burns on the back, and most of what they were dealing with seemed second degree, rather than third. Some of the burns were covered with dressings.

If, Dr. Caruso kept saying. *If this happens, Mrs. Duvall . . . If that happens . . .*

He spoke slowly, carefully, but I had to ask him to repeat what exactly had been burned. He didn't seem to mind repeating. "I've given you the number thirty-six," he said, "because the percentage — the extent, in other words — is crucial when we're talking about survival." He said that the other thing I had to keep in mind was the depth of the burn. A first degree is superficial, and heals all by itself in a matter of days, like sunburn. A second degree goes deeper — what they call "partial thickness" — and the third degree destroys the skin all the way through.

I asked him if Vincent's burns were second or third degree. The word *destroys* had seemed so blunt and cruel.

"Some of both," he said, "But remember, a second degree burn can take a long time to heal too. And the scarring is always an issue."

Like an aftershock, I remembered the boy with the amputation, and meanwhile I missed what the doctor was saying about the survival stage. "The survival stage?" I asked, interrupting him in the middle of something else.

"Yes. That's what we call it."

For the briefest moment it seemed like good news: Vincent had passed some milestone and was now considered a survivor.

"The first couple weeks are critical," he was saying. "Medicine is never an exact science, but with burns — well, with burns you can't safely predict anything. Your son is surviving one day at a time."

And so I realized that the word *survivor* hadn't actually been spoken, and my mind swerved back to the boy with the amputation, because I hadn't seen Vincent's hands, which had been hidden under the tent of sheets. "Are his hands all right?" I asked.

"The burns on the hands are significant," he said. "He could lose the tips of his fingers. He could lose more. I hope not, but I can't say for sure."

He was sitting still, with his own fingertips pressed together. It appeared he had all the time in the world to give, but I was so overwhelmed and tongue-tied. I tried to remember the questions that Mary Kate had drilled into me on the way to the airport.

I could hear the whir of a helicopter in the distance. "I don't really know what happened," I said. "No one told me how he got hurt in the first place."

He shook his head. "There was enemy fire, and they went down. That's all I know. The pilot died. Apparently the other troops had relatively minor injuries. At least they weren't sent to us here."

"The pilot died?"

"Before we could get him out of Japan. He was burned over eighty per cent."

Thirty-six. Vincent's number was less than half the pilot's. "I'm so sorry," I said.

"I'm sorry too, Mrs. Duvall."

Afterwards, I found Vincent sleeping under his tent of sheets, his head turned in such a way I might have fooled myself into thinking he'd suffered nothing worse than a little scrape, like the brush-burn he got when he fell off his bike in the alley behind the A & P.

It's terrible to be sitting on a burn ward with nothing to do, while the urgency whirls around you — carts and stretchers rolling back and forth, nurses and corpsmen and doctors stepping quickly about, not even meeting your eye. I got my rosary out from my pocketbook and began to pray: *Hail Mary, full of grace . . . Holy Mary, mother of God.* I kept my hands in my lap, with the rosary tucked out of sight, in case Vincent should wake up. I didn't want him to think I was afraid.

On the other side of the partition, in the second ward, someone was moaning. The sound was so constant and rhythmic it seemed mechanical. It occurred to me it might not be a person moaning after all, but rather a machine. A corpsman went around the partition and said something sharp that I couldn't make out. The moaning stopped. But a few seconds after the corpsman went away, the moaning started up again, as constant and rhythmic as it had been before.

Hail Mary, full of grace. In my head, the marching boys answered — *Box me up and send me home* — and from further back in my head, the chanting protestors on the evening news, my own daughter Mary Kate somewhere among them, in danger of getting arrested — *Bring them home! Bring them home!*

Well, Vincent was home now, I told myself, or at least home in America.

Tears came to my eyes. Another helicopter passed overhead, flying low, and I thought of the taxi driver's nephew, Carlos the warrant officer. I pictured him handsome and carefree, his limbs intact, his hands as strong and healthy as they'd been the day he was born. What did he know of the burn ward, while he was flying around above the trees of Vietnam? What did his taxi driver uncle know — or his mother, waiting at home for it all to be over, counting the days?

Box me up and send me home . . . And moving backwards to the first line — *If I die.*

If this happens, Mrs. Duvall . . . If that happens.

I prayed then: for Vincent and the other boys on that cramped little ward, for Carlos, for the marching recruits, and also for the young man at the airport, the kind one with the ruined face.

3

"I've got to get out of this house," Frank said.

It was a Sunday morning in 1954. A few days earlier he'd been fired for drinking on the job at Bethlehem Steel.

I was cleaning up after breakfast. The children were running around upstairs, and we were all going to be late for the 9:00 Mass.

"Please, Frank," I said. "Don't do this." What I meant was don't go off on a binge, because I needed him to be there — and be sober — for Mary Kate's birthday party that afternoon. The whole family was coming over, and a few of Mary Kate's friends. I had decorated the cake like a carousel, with animal crackers mounted on drinking straws all around the edge.

"I'm so goddamned miserable I don't know what to do with myself," he said.

I put a hand on his shoulder, and felt him flinch from it. "Everything will be all right," I said.

"You never give up, do you?" he said. "You're miserable too, but you won't admit it. Everything will be all right — You're like a broken record."

"I'm not miserable," I said. "I'm just trying to hold things together here — for you, and for the children."

"Because you have to. Because the Holy Catholic Church says you have to. You should have booted me out a long time ago, but no, you keep hanging on like a goddamned little martyr. Saint Mary Katherine Duvall. Christ — Why can't you just let go?"

Steady — that was how I drove the children to church that day, passing the familiar faces of the houses along Constance Avenue, and the Hennessey's two dogwoods in bloom on the corner, the white petals shining like light on the surface of water. It seemed to me that I was fighting toward that surface for breath.

Frank was not there for the birthday party. He was gone for nearly six months, and half the time I didn't know where he was. In the mean time he cleaned out our savings account. I had to go to my father-in-law and ask him to make the mortgage payments.

"You can have whatever you need, Kitty," my father-in-law said. "But make sure you put it where Frank can't get his hands on it." The poor old man was so ashamed, standing there on the front porch, holding his hat in his hand while Vincent rode his tricycle back and forth on the sidewalk.

There were long-distance phone calls from Frank — sad, three-minute calls in which he'd ask about the children one by one. He'd say he had a good job lined up in West Virginia or Ohio or whatever state he was calling from. Then the operator would cut in, and our time would be up.

When he did come home, he promised to make things right. But I knew that from then on he'd always be on the verge of tearing away. I saw it in his face, when he was working around the house — fixing a spigot, cleaning out the gutters — a look that said it wasn't worth his effort, because it was all a lost cause.

There were good times, like the Friday nights when he'd drive us all out to the snowball stand on Joppa Road, the one with so many flavors Vincent would sometimes cry trying to make up his mind. And that summer he built the tree house, when he was out there with his toolbox and a jar of iced tea, the three children and half the kids on the block watching his every move. I never did see fit to take that tree house down, not even the year I threw the big party for Mary Kate, when she graduated from college.

But with Frank, the good times were so short-lived. At any moment his mood could darken, and then there would be anger to deal with — days of brooding, followed by attacks against me, for there was always something about me that set him off. He seldom drank in my presence. He'd just get angry all of sudden, and then he'd disappear.

As soon as Vincent was in first grade, I took a secretarial job in the office at St. Anthony's. My mother helped me, looking after the children when they came home from school. Frank's mother was long dead, but his Father supported us. He wasn't a wealthy man, but he was certainly comfortable, and he saw to it that we didn't lose the house, and that the children stayed in Catholic school. When my own father died of cancer, Frank didn't even make it to the funeral.

For better or worse, until death . . . Sometimes, without warning, I'd fall into this dark daydream: the phone ringing and some far-away stranger informing me that Frank was dead — a car crash in which he never knew what hit him, or a heart attack that had taken him in his sleep. I felt guilty about these dreams, and would immediately pray to God that I hadn't meant it. I loved Frank. But somehow I'd separated the man who came home from the War in the Pacific to hold me in his arms in the dark, from the one who took off in the car we hadn't finished paying for. It was almost as though the man I married really had died.

Eventually Frank settled in Florida. He came to see the children now and then, usually bearing gifts — once a pink sweater for Mary Kate that was a couple sizes too small, another time baseballs for the boys, autographed by a major league player he said he'd met in a restaurant in Georgia.

I never filed for divorce. As far as the Catholic Church was concerned, my marriage to Frank was cast in stone. I made do, as though being left to raise three children alone were an accident to be endured with as much dignity as I could muster, not unlike the arrival of a change-of-life baby. In the family and among friends, it was understood that Frank's leaving was something beyond my control, but a disgrace nevertheless. No one would be so unkind as to bring it up in polite conversation.

But one time my brother-in-law Richard came over to the house — by himself, one evening after supper — asking if we might have a little talk. I sent the children upstairs to do their homework, and Richard sat down at the dining room table and gave me an awkward smile.

"You need to get some legal advice, Kitty," he said, looking me in the eye. "You need to file for a separation."

Richard wasn't a Catholic, but he knew enough to avoid the word *divorce*. He tried to make a legal separation sound like nothing worse than taking out an insurance policy. "You'd just be looking after yourself and the kids," he said

I told him I'd think about it, and I did. A couple weeks later I got as far as asking the priest in confession.

"I see nothing sinful in what you're describing," this priest whispered through the screen, "as long as the marriage vows are held sacred. It would be a wise to protect the financial welfare of your children."

He was a young priest, just out of seminary and new to St. Anthony's. About a month later, he disappeared from the parish, and word went around that he'd left the priesthood to get married. So much for his understanding of vows, I thought, and I took it as a sign.

And so the legal separation got put on the back burner. When my father-in-law died, he left everything in a trust for the children, and that money was safe from Frank anyway.

Out of the blue, shortly before Vincent left for Vietnam, Frank called to say he'd moved again, and to give me his phone number. He said he was sober, and going to A.A., getting himself straightened out. I'd heard all that before, and paid it little mind. He asked for Vincent's A.P.O. address. He said he wanted to write to Vincent, maybe even send a package. Before I could even take it in, he veered off on a different course. "By the way," he said. "I've been thinking that we should talk about a divorce."

I was taken aback. I actually laughed, though it certainly wasn't funny. "I'm still a practicing Catholic, Frank," I said. "Remember?"

"Yeah, I remember," he said, laughing softly too. "How could I forget? But the thing is, I'm not — a practicing Catholic, I mean. So will you at least think about it?"

I said I couldn't be thinking about that right then, not with Vincent on my mind.

❍

Colonel Anderson made the arrangements for me to stay in the guesthouse. There was a young soldier standing there, already holding my suitcase in one hand, and a brown paper bag in the other. The Colonel introduced him as Corporal Allen, and said he would drive me over to the guesthouse.

She pointed to the brown bag. "I packed you a little something to eat," she said. "Tomorrow we'll see to it that you get a meal card, so you can use the mess hall."

Corporal Allen drove me in a military car, even though the guesthouse was so close by I could have walked it in two minutes. The guesthouse looked a bit like a dormitory, and later I learned that it was originally a dormitory for nurses. Across the road was a row of the yellow houses with red tile roofs, smaller than the houses I saw on the way in. There were swing sets and tricycles in the yards.

Corporal Allen carried my suitcase and led the way inside, down the hall on the first floor. "Here you are, ma'am," he said, opening the door so I could go in ahead of him.

It was a surprisingly bright room. There were twin beds made up tight in simple green cord spreads, two ladder-back chairs, two dressers — good solid furniture, but so plain against the pale green walls, and not one picture. Except for the two beds, it was about what I'd always imagined a convent cell would look like.

Corporal Allen put the brown bag on the dresser and the suitcase on one of the beds. He opened another door, to show me there was a bathroom. "Is there anything I can get you, ma'am?"

I thanked him, and let him go, and then I went out to the pay phone in the hall to call Mary Kate at her apartment.

Her phone barely rang once before she picked up.

"He's all right," I said quickly, to put her mind at rest.

"Thank God," she said. "Oh Mom, I've been so scared."

Mary Kate had protested against the war the whole time she was in college, and after graduation she'd kept it up. When Vincent was drafted, her anger became a force to reckon with. Once she snapped at me as though I were to blame. *Think, Mom,* she said. *It's like you're asleep. They take our Vinnie and you don't say a word?* But now her voice was barely recognizable, a little-girl voice from long ago. "Does he have burns on his face?"

"No, thank God."

"What about his hands?"

"Well, yes — His hands are burned, but the doctor says we'll just have to wait and see."

I tried to convey all the doctor's words clearly, but I deliberately left out the part about Vincent surviving a day at a time. I realized I couldn't picture precisely where all the burns were, and didn't remember how it all added up to thirty-six per cent. I was tired, and suddenly wanted nothing but to lie down.

I asked her to make some phone calls — Jack, my mother, my sister Bonnie. I told her I'd call again in the morning, when I had more to tell.

"OK," she said. "But Mom, I'm making plans to come down there — "

"Let's wait and see how things go," I said, cutting her off, because I couldn't begin to think about that.

Afterwards, I sat a moment in the phone booth. Up until that point, I'd put off calling Frank, but now it seemed wrong to have left him out. After all, he was the father, and had a right to be informed that his son had been badly hurt.

I had his new number in my wallet. I made the call collect.

A woman with a sweet, high-pitched voice answered, and for a moment I thought I'd dialed wrong. But the woman accepted the charges, and after a moment Frank got on.

"I'm in San Antonio," I said, as straightforward as I could, "at Brooke Army Medical Center. They've evacuated Vincent. He got hurt in a helicopter crash."

"Jesus Christ," he said, and then there was a fumbling noise, like maybe he'd lost control of the phone.

"Are you there, Frank?"

"I'm here. Have you seen him? Is he all right?"

I gave him the same report I gave Mary Kate. I took my time with it, all the while braced for some sort of angry thrashing from him, because Frank could get really angry, and physical too. He had once punched a hole in the kitchen door the size of a baking potato. But there was mostly silence on the other end of line.

"Are you all right, Frank?"

"How can I be all right?" he said quietly. "I'm sick about this. What should I do? Do you want me to come?"

I was sure he didn't mean it, but still it was unsettling to picture how it would be if he did come, how I'd have to prop him up the whole time and be constantly worried he'd have a bottle hidden on him somewhere, how he'd surely make a scene. "No, I don't think you need to do that," I said, "not right now," but I had a lump in my throat — that I was alone in Fort Sam Houston with the wounded child, and there was no one there to comfort me.

I got a grip on myself and said I had to get going.

"I understand," he said quietly, almost tenderly. "You go ahead, Kitty."

Back in the room, I looked in the bag the Colonel had given me, and found a ham sandwich and an apple. On the way in I'd spotted a kitchenette, and went down there and put the bag in the refrigerator, because I couldn't imagine eating a thing.

I unpacked, and hung my good navy linen dress in the closet. I'd brought a hat — a white straw with a bunch of cherries at the band — and I put that up on the shelf.

Mary Kate had laughed when she saw I'd packed a hat. "What do you want a hat for, Mom?"

"For Mass on Sunday," I said.

And of course she rolled her eyes.

On the plane I'd worn my brand-new olive green knit, which I'd made myself from a Vogue pattern and had finished hemming only a week before I got the news about Vincent. When I stepped out of it and hung in the closet, it looked tired and worn-out already.

I took a good look at myself in the mirror over the dresser: pale round face, lipstick long gone, and a short round figure pulled together tidily by the right undergarments. Below the prominent eyebrows, my own green eyes stared back. It looked as though my hair hadn't seen a brush in days.

I inherited my mother's hair, not only the auburn color but also the stubborn thickness that resisted any style other than just plain curly. There was already some gray in it, or rather a yellowed white, like the color of old table linens. My sister Bonnie had been fussing about it. "Get yourself a bottle of Clairol, Kitty," she said. "You've got Mother's hair, but that doesn't mean you have to look as old as she is."

Even Mary Kate had been in favor of the Clairol, which seemed to me a contradiction, since she was the self-proclaimed feminist, the one always saying that women were too concerned about how men wanted them to look, too uncomfortable with their own bodies and so forth.

I dug the hairbrush from the suitcase and did some quick work with it. When I set it down on the dresser top, it looked peculiarly vulnerable there all by itself, in front of the plain mirror reflecting the bare walls. In my bedroom at home there were snapshots of the children tucked into the mirror, and an old construction paper valentine from Vincent, on which he'd written in crayon: *My mom's name is Kitty. She is very pretty.* That was a special valentine to me, unlike the cards they made at school under the direction of the nuns. The nuns were inclined to hand out mimeographed drawings of flowers, and verses about the Blessed Mother, so that in the end the children carried home a version of the good Catholic woman that could hardly have matched up with their own mothers. But Vincent's valentine began with my name. I was as delighted as he must have been, to find my name rhymed with "pretty."

It was all I could do then to brush my teeth and get into my nightgown. After I pulled back the stiff, antiseptic-smelling sheets and got in the bed, I remembered my rosary. I'd left it in the pocket of my dress, and had to get up and feel for it in the dark.

4

December 1, 1968 was the last time we were all together before Vincent left for Vietnam. It was my mother's seventieth birthday, and also the first Sunday in Advent. Vincent was home on leave. He and Jack had been out late the night before — a going-away party Vincent's friends had cooked up — so I let them sleep until the last minute. When I went into their room to raise the shade, Vincent groaned and pulled the pillow over his head.

Jack laughed. "Hey soldier boy," he said, "you didn't think she'd let you off from Mass, did you?"

But they were out of bed in time, and stood elbowing each other at the bathroom mirror, Vincent pink and shining with his hair cut close to the scalp, Jack dark and scruffy in his long hair and half-grown mustache.

Vincent wore his uniform.

On the way to church I stopped to pick up my mother, as always. When Vincent got out of the car, and strode forward to help his grandmother, she took his elbow and beamed up at him like a star-struck girl. "Look at my handsome grandson," she said.

We waited for Mary Kate in the vestibule, but as usual she was late. The priest was already on the altar by the time she came breezing in, looking like she'd just jumped out of the shower, her hair still damp and caught back into a loose ponytail. She was wearing a very short skirt, and white summer pumps. Her legs were bare.

"You'll catch your death," I whispered to her. "Where's your coat?"

She hugged her grandmother and kissed her on the cheek. "Happy birthday, Nana." When she turned to Vincent, her eyes filled with tears. "Hey, Vinnie. Look at you!" she said, and threw her arms around his middle. The other latecomers hurrying in had to squeeze past them to get by.

"Jeez," Vincent said. "Control yourself."

St. Anthony's was always packed for the eleven o'clock Mass. I thought we were going to have to stand, except for my mother of course, but then the usher — Jim Carpenter, who was once Vincent's Cub Scout leader — marched down the aisle and made everyone slide over in the pews. Jack and Vincent sat with their grandmother in the very first pew. Mary Kate and I squeezed into the pew behind. I was struck by how small my mother looked, propped between the two grandsons like a blue-haired doll.

To tell the truth, as I sat there looking at my children, I actually had hope for the future. There was Mary Kate, graduated from college already, supporting herself in a little apartment on Calvert Street with a good job copyediting at the *Baltimore Sun*. There was Jack, studying hard at Loyola College and preparing to take the exams for medical school. And Vincent — Seeing him there, so handsome and manly in his uniform, was like slipping a brand new photograph into the frame, right on top of the old one. Underneath, out of view, was that sad picture of the younger Duvall boy, who could have been a star basketball player if he hadn't gotten into trouble.

I opened my missal and saw the pamphlet tucked inside, something I'd picked up from the racks in the vestibule months ago. *The Rosary — An Urgent Appeal for Peace*. I prayed that God would protect Vincent in Vietnam. I pushed the fear to the back of my mind. Two years in the Army, and actually 6 months of that behind us already: We could survive it. Vincent would come home with a sense of accomplishment, go off to college, graduate, get a good job. Everything would be all right.

❍

The first morning at Fort Sam Houston, I woke up with my heart racing, because I'd been dreaming about a baby again — a dream that kept coming back, since even before Vincent left for Vietnam. The baby in these dreams wasn't Mary Kate or Jack or Vincent. Nevertheless, in the dream he was unquestionably mine, and the frightening part was that I'd forgotten about him — forgotten to feed him for days, forgotten to take him to the doctor for the vaccinations, forgotten the poor little thing had ever been born.

This time I dreamed the baby was lying in the laundry basket, down in the basement by the washing machine of all places. He didn't make a sound, but just gazed up at me, starved and vacant-eyed, even as I was lifting him into my arms. My next-door neighbor Alma Henderson was convinced that baby dreams had to do with maternal anxiety. My sister Bonnie said it was probably just change of life.

After I woke up, I could still feel the pressure of that little rag-doll body against my breasts. It had all seemed so real. I had to lie there and count the children in my head: *Mary Kate, Jack, Vincent, each one nursed and fed.*

It was a dark morning, with thunder rumbling in the distance. After I got myself dressed and ready to go, I looked through the blinds, and saw the sooty clouds on the horizon beyond the hospital, a strip of blue on the underside — too blue, exactly the color of a gas flame. I was glad I'd remembered to pack an umbrella.

As I headed across the parking lot, the wind was beginning to blow, making a restless, scratching sound through the palm trees. The thunder rumbled again, closer this time. I hurried up the steps of the hospital, and saw that the pigeons were huddled up there on the ledge, above the Latin I couldn't translate.

On the fourth floor, I washed my hands and put on the gown, the way Colonel Anderson had taught me. But when I got to the ward, Vincent wasn't there. His bed had been stripped to the mattress, the sheets balled up at the foot. The little nurse I'd been introduced to — Lieutenant Bukowsky — was wiping the bedside table with a wet rag.

"You're a little early," she said. "He's back in the tank room." The rag hung limply from her hand, suspended in action. "Are you staying at the guesthouse, Mrs. Duvall?"

The patient in the corner waved at me. "You can come over and visit with me, ma'am," he said, laying on the charm in a heavy drawl. He was sitting in a big wooden wheelchair, a very handsome young man, a little older than Vincent. His legs were propped straight in front, and he wore a towel across his lap. Urine ran from the catheter to the bag hanging near the wheel of his chair. From the toes clear up to the thighs, he was wrapped in dressings. "I'm Pete Christie," he said.

"Kitty Duvall," I said. "Vincent's mother. How do you do?"

"Not bad. Considering."

Lieutenant Bukowsky stepped forward. "I think maybe Mrs. Duvall might want to go to the canteen for a cup of coffee, Lieutenant Christie," she said firmly.

He winked at me. "The boss lady has a better idea. I guess I'll be seeing you later."

I glanced around then at the others — most out of their beds now, some in wheelchairs, some up and about in baggy bathrobes, or pajama bottoms. Jimmy, the one the Colonel had spoken to the day before, was lying on his side, reading a comic book.

Suddenly there was a loud and terrible cry. And then another, followed by choking sobs.

"Let me tell you how to get to the canteen, Mrs. Duvall," the lieutenant said. She dropped her rag onto the cart. "Come on out to the desk with me, and I'll tell you how to get there."

But I was listening for the next cry. I needed to know if it was Vincent. I had a good hold on the cold, metal foot of the bed. "What do they do in the tank room?" I asked.

"The tank is like a big bathtub — a Hubbard tank. The patients soak in the water. We have to remove the skin that won't heal. The soaking helps. Did the doctor explain about debridement?"

He had. Who would forget an ugly word like *debridement*?

The sobbing started up again, and then a stretcher was coming, one corpsman at the front pulling, another at the back pushing. The sobbing was moving toward me through the ward. I saw then that it wasn't Vincent on the stretcher, but someone else's boy, sobbing still, not like he was in pain now, but like his heart had been broken. His legs were exposed. The skinned flesh was red and glistening, red as a side of beef.

I glanced over at Pete Christie. He closed his eyes, shook his head.

The lieutenant came to the foot of Vincent's bed. I could only stare at the freckles on her pale forearm, at her small hand resting on the foot of the bed near mine. I saw she wore a wedding band — startling, because it had seemed to me she was just a girl, though she was probably older than I was when I got married.

"It would be better if you waited in the canteen, Mrs. Duvall," she said softly. "Have you had breakfast? You could get a cup of coffee, and maybe a muffin or something."

I was thinking of the brown bag Colonel Anderson had given me. I was thinking it was peculiar how these people on the burn ward were always sending you off to eat. But in truth I'd put nothing on my stomach since the small dry sandwich on the plane.

The lieutenant led me out past the hubbub of the nurses' station, past two corpsmen standing by the dressing cart, one saying to the other, "We've got ourselves another screamer." *Screamer*. The word imbedded itself in my heart like a mean sliver of glass.

"Have you seen Major Trainer, the chaplain?" the lieutenant asked, when we got to the elevator. "He was asking about you. And Father Smith — You're Catholic, aren't you?"

Extreme Unction, the sacrament of the dying — Had they felt it necessary to anoint Vincent?

The lieutenant smiled hesitantly. "Are you OK?" She touched me lightly on the arm. "Please. You can call me Ann."

Downstairs in the canteen, I ordered a cup of coffee. The woman who waited on me — and older woman, a volunteer probably — reminded me of my mother. She had powdered her soft, wrinkled cheeks with perfect circles of rouge, and she wore an old-fashioned embroidered handkerchief pinned to her bosom. When she set the cup in front of me, there was something about the way she hesitated — as though she recognized a need in me for particular attention — that was almost treacherous.

My son has been badly burned. I could imagine saying that to her, falling apart right there in the canteen, and how she would come around from behind the counter to wrap me up in those soft fleshy arms.

"You want some help carrying that to the table, honey?" she asked.

I kept my eyes on her pretty handkerchief. I said I'd be fine.

And meanwhile Vincent was in a big bathtub, and someone was cutting away his skin. And was he screaming?

Water. I had a sudden memory of the two boys, Jack and Vincent, playing with their plastic boats in the bathtub until their little fingers were wrinkled and the water was stone cold. I had such a pain in my throat I couldn't swallow.

Rain was hitting hard against the windows, and there was a rumble of thunder and a flicker of lightning. I sat at a table in the corner, and from there I watched the comings and goings of strangers, most of them in uniform — medals and stripes, bars and eagles and stars both large and small. I made a little game of figuring out what they all meant — the eagles were for the colonels, like Colonel Anderson. On the other lapel nearly all of them wore the medical symbol — the staff with the snake entwined around.

I got my notepad from my pocketbook, and read down the lists I'd made at home. Everything had been crossed out but *Water houseplants.* What had possessed me to think of the plants? But there they were, right below *Pay phone bill.* I longed for that busyness now. It was awful to sit and think, to stare at my own hand, holding the pen. It was then I saw the little brown scar on my wrist, and remembered burning myself on the iron, running to hold my whole arm under the cold water at the sink, and how for days after, whenever I reached into the oven or lifted a lid from a pan on the stove, I'd be conscious of that burning, just above the wrist. *Thirty-six per cent.* How could a person take that much pain?

I started a list of names: *Colonel Anderson, Lieutenant Ann Bukowsky, Major Caruso, Jimmy, Pete Christie.* A list can be a comfort, something to hold onto, like a rosary. I added the chaplain, *Major Trainer*, even though I hadn't met him yet, and the priest, *Father Smith.*

I waited an hour. When I returned to the ward, Vincent was sitting up in a chair, and I had the full view: the dead-white ointment — Sulfamylon — spread thick on one side of his neck, his shoulders, his chest, a few spots here and there near the waist. His arms were wrapped in thick dressings, but his hands, resting against splints, were left half exposed. His fingers were white and stiffly swollen, horrifying little clubs.

I said hello and just stood there, gripping my pocketbook like an awkward guest.

"Hi, Mom." He was trembling with a chill. They had set two heat lamps to shine directly at him, and the Sulfamylon was wet and glistening in the light. He didn't really look me in the eye.

A corpsman appeared with a meal tray — an older man, about my age. His graying hair was cut in a flattop. He wore a scrub suit, just like the other corpsmen, but I was certain that his real uniform had lots of stripes. The name on his tag was Berry. He was a sergeant surely, and it was clear he was really in charge, more so than the nervous little lieutenant.

"Are you up to feeding him, Mom?" Berry asked, pulling up a chair.

"Yes, I'm up to it." I set my pocketbook on the bedside table, as though I knew what I was doing, and sat down in front of the breakfast tray.

He abandoned me without a word, and went about setting up another patient's tray.

I lifted the cover from Vincent's plate. They'd sent him tea, chicken broth, scrambled eggs and toast, gelatin, and some sort of sherbet in a sodden cup — a strange breakfast. "Well," I said as brightly as I could.

"This looks good."

"Is the sherbet pink or green?" Vincent asked.

"Pink. Would you like some?"

"I must be dying. I can have dessert first."

I was so delighted he'd made a little joke. I laughed out loud. He gave me a rueful smile, but the effort of it cost him a fit of shivering.

"Are you cold?" I asked.

He didn't answer. His eyes were all over the place, never really lighting anywhere.

"You got to eat, buddy," Pete called from the corner. Pete had no burns on his hands. His plate was nearly clean already. "That's real important. You eat good, and in a couple of days they'll let you go out for lunch at Earl Abel's, you and your mom. You can get yourself a nice big hamburger."

Sergeant Berry was passing the foot of the bed with a stack of linens. He shook his head. "You're not going to be eating out any time soon, son. You've got to eat what they put in front of you. Everything on that tray."

Pete rolled his eyes behind the sergeant's back and winked at me.

Vincent wasn't really paying attention to any of this. His hands were lying still, on either side of the tray. It was my job to get the sherbet to his mouth — the only job they had given me. Suddenly I was thrown back into the alarm of the baby dream: I hadn't been paying attention, had neglected to feed my own child.

I plunged the spoon into the sherbet. Vincent opened his mouth. How many days had he been eating like that, dependent on others, on strangers, to fill his mouth? But no more, for now they had given me a job. Thank God for that job.

In between spoonfuls I chattered in my usual way — describing my room in the guesthouse, telling him how quickly it had stormed in the morning, how strange it was to have a palm tree right outside my window. Vincent had nothing to say. Sometimes he'd nod, but mostly he seemed anxious to get the eating out of the way. When he had eaten less than half his meal, the trembling got worse.

"What's the matter, Vinnie?" Such a stupid question, but at least it brought Sergeant Berry over.

"Finish this broth here, soldier," he said, "and then we'll get you to bed." He held the cup to Vincent's lips as though he expected no objection, and Vincent was more or less forced to drink it all down.

When Vincent stood, Sergeant Berry held him by the small of the back, grabbing a fist of his pajama bottoms because there was really no place to grab hold on his arms, no place that wasn't covered with Sulfamylon.

I stood up too, but my knees were shaking, so I sat down again, in front of the half-eaten breakfast.

"Nice and easy, son," Sergeant Berry said.

"Yeah, take it easy there, Vince, " Pete said. "You'll be O.K."

Vincent hobbled toward the bed, his arms held out, stiff as a plastic doll's.

When he was settled under his tent of sheets again, I went and kissed him on the forehead.

He didn't open his eyes. He barely murmured goodbye.

Downstairs, emerging from the hospital, I found the skies had cleared. Steam rose from the sidewalk. On the hospital lawn I saw a flock of big black birds — crows maybe, but different from the crows at home, bigger. I was catching my breath in the oppressive heat, watching those big birds pace self-importantly back and forth below the palm trees, when a sturdy-looking man in a khaki uniform came striding toward me, whistling a perky tune. He stopped when he noticed me. "You wouldn't be Mrs. Duvall, would you?"

I saw the cross on his lapel, and the nametag — *Trainer.* He had a wide easy smile. He shook my hand warmly, and introduced himself as "Hal Trainer, chaplain." I saw from the gold on his other lapel that he was a major, like Dr. Caruso.

"I've been trying to catch up with you since yesterday," he said.

"I'm sorry," I said. "I've either been on the ward or in the guesthouse."

"It's not your fault," he said. "I'm the one who's running around. How are you getting along?"

I said I was doing all right, and he apologized he didn't have time to talk just then, because they were waiting for him up on the ward. He handed me a card and said I could call him any time, night or day. Then he strode away, taking a short cut across the wet grass, no concern for his spit-shined shoes. Those big black birds lifted themselves from his path, and settled beneath the next tree.

5

At one time, back in the fifties, our house on Constance Avenue looked exactly like every other house on the block — a small, brown-shingled bungalow with a covered porch. But by the end of the sixties that house was unique, simply because it was the only house that hadn't changed. Over the years, up and down the block, the other houses sprouted dormers and additions and big decks out back. The Hendersons next door tacked on a two-story aluminum-sided addition without much concern for making it match. When I stood at the kitchen sink, I still looked directly at Alma Henderson's window, but Alma wasn't looking back at me from her sink anymore, because they had shifted the kitchen into the new part.

Frank and I moved into that house as newly-weds, and it was understood we would sell in three or four years, because back then Frank had big ideas about buying a piece of property out in Dulaney Valley. But in three or four years it was clear to me what a struggle it would be just to hold onto what little house we had, because by then Frank was drinking heavily, losing jobs regularly.

Sometimes when I was out in the yard, hanging the wash on the line — years later, when Frank was gone — I'd look over at the Hendersons' and give thanks for what I had. I was glad I hadn't cut down a beautiful maple tree to make room for a big ugly addition, and that there had always been a decent-sized yard for the children to run around in when they were small, even if they did have to grow up in a broken family.

I was devoted to that house on Constance Avenue, but not in the way my neighbor Alma Henderson was devoted to hers. Alma was always poring over interior decorating magazines. She even took a part-time job in a florist shop, just to pay for her new slipcovers and draperies. Alma took pride in how the house was dressed up, how it showed. But for me it was more about the space itself — from the well outside the cellar door, where the mint came up so happily every year, to the crawlspace under the eaves. Each nook and corner was dear to me in a way I could never have explained.

○

At suppertime, I was all set to make myself useful. Vincent was already up in the chair when I got there, and the corpsmen were bringing in the meal trays. There were fewer corpsmen and nurses around in the evening. The patients up and walking were helping the others with their trays.

I was pleased that Vincent was genuinely smiling, looking me in the eye.

"Perfect timing," Pete called from his corner, when I pulled up my chair. "I was getting ready to wheel over there and get him started," he said. "We make a good pair, don't we — Vince with the hands, and me with the feet?"

I opened the sugar packet and stirred it into Vincent's iced tea, and caught myself thinking that at least Pete had the use of his hands, and wishing crazily that Vincent's feet had been burned instead. I looked across at the boy who had lost his leg. I tried not to look too much at Vincent's fingers. They were so stiff and swollen they didn't look real.

I propped the straw in exactly the right position so Vincent could reach it, and while he was drinking I looked over at Pete. Beside him on the bedside table he had a photograph of a pretty girl with her dark hair teased up in a beehive hairdo. It was the typical graduation photograph — the bare shoulders above the black drape, the expression serious.

"My fiancée," Pete said, as though he'd been waiting for me to notice.

"A very pretty girl," I said.

"You bet. She'll be here this weekend. She drives down from Austin."

"So you're from Texas?" I asked.

"Born and raised."

Vincent had finished half of his tea. I offered him some broth, and he took it on the spoon. After three spoonfuls, he surprised me by joining in.

"We got people from all over," he said. "Guys from the Navy and the Air Force too. See that guy over there?" He nodded in the direction of the one in the corner whose face was burned. "He's a marine."

The tremor was gone from his voice. It was so good to hear him talk. I tried to pace myself in offering the soup.

They had sent him meatloaf, mashed potatoes, and a big wedge of watermelon."Look, Vinnie," I said. "Watermelon."

Pete gave a short laugh. "We're up to our eyeballs in watermelon around here," he said. "We get it two times a day." He went on to tell me that there had been an article in the San Antonio paper about the burn unit, and in this article a doctor had said something about fluids being good for burns. Apparently a local farmer had seen the article and immediately donated a whole truckload of watermelons.

"I guess it was a patriotic gesture," I said.

"Yeah. A whole truckload of patriotism," Pete said. "You can't very well freeze watermelon. So eat up, Vince. There's more where that came from."

But Vincent only took a bite or two, and then he didn't want any more. His mood got dark as quickly as it had brightened a minute earlier.

I pushed the tray to the side for a while. I tried to keep the conversation going, but he interrupted me.

"Can you get my Orioles hat, Mom?" he said.

I was confused. "That hat must be at home, Vinnie. Remember?"

He was suddenly angry, veering from the hat to his friend Dennis, wanting to know why he hadn't shown up. I had to remind him that Dennis was back in Baltimore too.

Ann Bukowsky appeared, with a corpsman in tow, and they put him back to bed.

"He's tired, Mrs. Duvall," Ann said. "It's been a long day."

I put a hand on Vincent's head. His hair was growing in fuzzy, like the wiffle cut he used to get at Sal's Barber Shop on Belair Road when he was a little boy. And then I remembered how he had looked that morning at the airport, when he left for Vietnam — crisp as a new dollar bill in his uniform, a good sharp crease in his trousers. And I'd ironed those very trousers, waved goodbye, let him go.

Pete was studying me. "You take it easy now, Mrs. Duvall," he said. "Things'll look better in the morning. You'll see."

Curiously, he had used an old-time expression, a favorite of my own mother. *Things will look better in the morning, Kitty,* my mother would always say to me, when some sort of worry had me in knots.

There wasn't a shred of truth to that old-time expression, at least on the burn ward there wasn't. On the burn ward, it was just as likely things would look a lot worse in the morning.

"Goodbye, Pete," I said. "Look out for him, O.K.?"

"Yes, ma'am," he said. "You can count on it."

I went down to the mess hall for supper, stood in line, and told them what to spoon onto my plate.

"Potatoes, ma'am? Lyonnaised or mashed?" the young man called out from behind the steaming trays, keeping up his rhythm, singing it over and over as they moved along — *lyin' eyes or May ash, lyin' eyes or May ash* — like a drill sergeant, though he was probably just a private, just a kid about Vincent's age.

I caught a glimpse of myself in the mirrored partition at the end of the line: Kitty Duvall, age 45, who for most of her adult life had arranged the day around the preparation of meals for others, now had only to show up, and three meals a day would be placed in front of her — bland, institutional meals, but nourishing nevertheless.

That night I actually slept well, which was a good thing, because the next day wasn't going to be easy.

In the morning, when I arrived on the ward, Corporal Jenks stepped away from his cart and flagged me down. He was a big fellow who looked like he ought to be playing football, not pushing a laundry cart. "He's in the tank room right now, ma'am," he said, ducking his head, embarrassed. "I'm sorry. Visitors aren't allowed until after they're finished in the tank room."

Then I heard the screaming, and knew it was Vincent. I could tell Jenks knew it too.

"Go on now, ma'am," he said gently. "You can come back later." He moved the laundry cart forward a little, as though he thought it necessary to block my path.

I turned on my heel, for there was nothing to do but walk away from that screaming, out to the elevator and down, out the front door, where the hot air nearly knocked me over, like something animal. I walked as far as the parking lot and sat down on a bench in the broiling sun.

The tears kept coming. I found a handkerchief in my pocketbook. It was a thin little thing, a gift from one of the children years ago. *A lady always keeps a good linen handkerchief ready* — so my mother always said, but it made it worse to think of my mother, far away in Baltimore, probably watching "The Price is Right" on television, blessedly unaware that her grandchild Vinnie — her favorite, everyone could see that — was screaming in pain.

Suddenly someone sat down beside me: the chaplain, Major Trainer. "Mornings are rough, aren't they?" he said.

"Yes," I said, and wiped my face with the handkerchief. "They had him in the tank."

"Mornings are especially rough when you have to face the tanks." He leaned on his knees and smiled sidelong at me.

We sat in silence for a moment, looking in the same direction, across the parking lot at the hospital.

"I can't imagine what it's like when it's your own child," he said, "but I'll tell you one thing, I'll never forget how I felt the first time I stepped foot in this place. There was this soldier in the tank room. Big guy, standing there next to the tank without a stitch on, and crying like a little kid. It about knocked me over — and here I was the chaplain, the one who's supposed to do the praying."

Major Trainer was a nice-looking man, with a wide, expressive mouth. I figured he was about my age, maybe a bit younger. His complexion was ruddy, pockmarked, but that made his eyes seem all the more blue. Kind eyes, kind smile — I didn't want him to stop talking.

He said no two people were going to react the same way. Some people got mad, and some people got frightened. He said he'd seen family members get so involved they made a pest of themselves with the nurses, and then others would freeze up and not make a move. "Personally, I think a good cry is healthy," he said.

He seemed to be waiting for me to say something back, but all I could manage was "Thank you."

He looked in the direction of the hospital. "Would it be all right if I read a little prayer?"

I said I'd appreciate that, and he took a small black book from his pocket, turned to a page marked with a slip of cardboard, and read a short prayer. I assumed it was Protestant, because I'd never heard it before. It began with *Heavenly Father*, and mentioned the needs of the sick and the wounded. It also mentioned the armed forces. There was one line that was familiar to me — the line about waiting for the Lord, *more than they that wait for the morning*.

"I understand you're Roman Catholic," he said, closing his book. "I want you to know that the priest, Father Smith, has already visited your son."

Out of the blue, a flock of those birds I'd seen the day before swooped to the ground in front of us, cawing bossily.

"Grackles," he said, as though he'd read my mind. "I think they call them jackdaws around here. Noisy aren't they?"

"Yes. But I'm kind of fascinated by them for some reason."

"Me too. What do you think it is about them?"

"I don't know. Maybe it's just the distraction."

"I think you've got something there," he said with a laugh. "So — You flew by yourself from Baltimore?"

I nodded, wondering if they had recorded somewhere in Vincent's records that his father was estranged.

"And are you settling in at the guesthouse?" he asked.

"Yes. It's very comfortable."

"Good, good. I'll warn you though, it can get lonely. You get caught up in the small world of the burn ward, and then when you step outside you feel a little disoriented sometimes."

"Mostly it's terrible to have nothing to do," I said.

"True. The busy ones are lucky in a way. Running around, saving lives all day, they don't have time to think." He put his book into his back pocket. "Would you like me to go back up to the ward with you?"

"Thank you," I said. "But I think I'll go back to the guesthouse for a while."

"That's probably a good idea," he said. "Give your son a little time to settle down."

"Right. He probably doesn't want me to see him like that."

He smiled at me, so kindly. "Don't get me wrong. It's a good thing you've done — coming here to be with him. I admire your strength, Mrs. Duvall. We all do."

I went back to the guesthouse and made my phone calls.

All along, while I was there, I made those calls — took my stack of quarters to the pay phone and called Mary Kate at her apartment, or Jack at home. Vincent was making progress, I kept saying, the doctor was pleased, it was just a matter of time. Why frighten them, when they were so far away, and helpless?

Sometimes I called my sister Bonnie. She'd insist I hang up and save the quarters, and then she'd call right back. "To hell with how much it's costing," she'd say. "Just go ahead and talk, Kit."

I would dispense with the report on Vincent, sparing her the details, and then she'd take over and rattle on about her kids and what they were having for dinner. I would picture her there in her kitchen — the wallpaper with all those tireless flower baskets reflecting yellow light, the wallpaper I'd helped to hang, the two of us cussing and laughing because it was hard to match the pattern and Bonnie hadn't bought enough rolls.

Sitting there in the phone booth, it seemed such a long time since I'd had a cup of coffee in my sister Bonnie's kitchen, at the table forever cluttered with newspapers and her latest decoupage project. Actually, it had only been a couple of weeks ago.

I called my mother too, but it was a strain. "Hello?" Mother would shout, as though the telephones were made of tin cans and string. "Is that you Kitty? Is Vincent all right? Gracious. You scared me half to death."

Once I called Frank, and the woman with the high-pitched voice answered. "Oh, hold on," the woman said anxiously. "I'll get him right away."

"Kitty?" Apparently Frank had been there at the woman's elbow. "Is everything all right?"

I gave him a good report, and he thanked me for it, warmly, as though I'd done him a big favor. The whole time we were on the phone, I could hear the sound of water in the background, and an occasional clatter. The woman was now washing up the dishes.

"So, how about this, Kitty?" Frank said. "When Vinnie gets home, how about I come up to Baltimore for a visit? Maybe take him out to a ball game or something like that?"

It caught me off guard. I'd half expected him to offer again to come to see Vincent on the burn ward. I was braced to argue against it. Instead he had tossed out the dream: father and son happily re-united in the bleachers at Memorial Stadium. I held onto it for a moment, that picture of Vincent well again, the thirty-six per cent entirely healed, and Frank clean as a whistle, buying hotdogs at the ballpark, but no beer.

"That would be nice," I said. "It'll be good for him to get out, I'm sure."

"So, are you doing OK yourself, Kitty?" he asked.

The dishwashing had stopped in the background. It was as though the room at the other end of the line waited for the answer.

"I'm OK," I said.
"That's good," he said, kindly. "I'm doing pretty good too."

6

New Year's Day, 1969. Jack had invited a couple of his friends from Loyola to the house to watch the football games. They were having a nice time, and I didn't want to get in the way, but I was determined to dismantle the Christmas tree and pack up every last decoration in the house.

"Do you mind, Jack?" I'd gotten out the boxes stuffed with tissue paper and newspaper. "I've just got to get this done."

He barely took his eyes off the television. "Go ahead. You won't bother us."

His two friends smiled congenially from the sofa, from behind the beer bottles sweating on the coasters, and the bowl of party mix I'd toasted for them in the oven.

It was satisfying work to wrap up the balls and ornaments in the yellowing tissue paper, to pull the strings of lights from the dry branches and gather up the figures of the manger scene. I couldn't wait to stuff it all back up in the attic. When the game was over, I'd get Jack to drag the tree out to the curb.

In fact, I couldn't wait to put away that entire bad year — 1968, the year Vincent was in Vietnam and missed Christmas entirely, the year that the sadness just kept coming at us out of the television: Martin Luther King dead, Bobby Kennedy dead, the heart-wrenching protests all over the county, college students out of control, veterans in their ragtag uniforms out of control, thousands and thousands of soldiers dead.

"The whole damned country going to hell in a hand basket" — that was how my brother-in-law Richard put it, in April of that year, when we were all together in front of the television, watching the streets of Baltimore go up in flames during the riots, the federal troops loading all those angry people into cattle trucks and carting them off to jail.

○

Rounds on the burn ward were a sight to see — A big herd of doctors moving in almost shoulder to shoulder, settling at the foot of one bed for a while, and then moving on to the next.

I counted them one day: two colonels, two lieutenant colonels, three majors, including our own Dr. Caruso, three captains, two civilians wearing surgical gowns over their street clothes. Colonel Anderson was at the front of the herd with her clipboard. The captains at the back had clipboards too.

The whole place seemed to shift when rounds came through, everything and every other person squeezed to the corners, out of their way. I had to scoot back in my chair when they arrived at Vincent's bed, even though I was practically against the wall already.

"Private First Class Vincent Duvall," Dr. Caruso said, and he nodded at me. "And his mother, visiting from Baltimore."

When he started running through the history, I couldn't keep up — *third degree component . . . homograft . . . spirometry . . . full-thickness*. Vincent kept his eyes on Dr. Caruso, even when the others were asking their questions and giving their opinions.

After his report, Dr. Caruso put his hand on my shoulder and said he'd see us later.

The herd moved to the next bed. "First Lieutenant Peter Christie," one of them said.

Pete wasn't there. Another one said something I couldn't catch. They wavered for a moment — a brief flurry of charts from the captains at the back — and moved on.

"I guess they still have Pete in the tank," I said to Vincent.

"They put him in the Cube," he said matter-of-factly.

"What happened?"

He only shrugged. That familiar cloud of irritation was passing over his face, and he called the corpsman over, so they'd put him back to bed.

As I was leaving, I saw Ann Bukowsky making her rounds in the other ward. She was so thin, hovering a moment at this intravenous bottle, that catheter bag — too thin, I was thinking, because when she raised an arm to adjust the drip you could see through the baggy sleeve of the scrub dress, straight across her collarbone to the other side. And too pale — It appeared she didn't spend any time outside in the bright Texas sunshine. I almost went up to her, to ask about Pete, but she looked so busy, I thought better of it.

Out in the waiting room there was nothing to do but stare out the window at the wide flat post, at the cars moving slowly along either side of the big field browning in the sun. At home I'd have been scrubbing the kitchen floor, weeding the beds out front, talking over the hedge to Alma Henderson. Or maybe I'd walk up to the Woodlea Bakery for some sticky buns. I pictured the girl plucking those buns from the tray in the case, settling them in a white box, tying the string.

Dr. Caruso appeared and asked me to come down to his office.

"So how are you doing, Mrs. Duvall?" he asked, when we were both sitting down.

"I'm getting along all right."

"That's good." He pressed his lips into that reserved smile I was getting to know, a kind smile, encouraging, but with something held back. "I wish I could tell you that Vincent is out of the woods, but it isn't as simple as that with burns."

"He isn't out of the woods?"

"Not yet. But he's got a lot going for him. He's young and he's fit. That's how it is with all the troops we get. They're in good shape, in their prime."

In his prime. It gave me a start to think that way about Vincent. He was my youngest, a boy barely out of high school.

Dr. Caruso leaned back in his chair. I noticed the shadows under his eyes, and wondered if he'd been called in the night before. He wore a wedding band. If he had children, they were probably little ones.

"So far," he said, "it appears there are no complications." But he went on to say that with burns it sometimes happens that just when you think you're out of the woods, suddenly you're not. Infection sets in. Burned tissue is dead tissue, and just naturally attracts infection. The blood supply is poor, so the antibiotics aren't always the miracles people think they are. So you never know. Things can change, dramatically.

"Is that what happened to Vincent's friend Pete?" I asked.

"Lieutenant Christie?" He shook his head. "Those burns were very dirty, Mrs. Duvall. He stepped in a booby trap of some sort. Something rigged with filth, probably human excrement. A lot of infection to deal with."

My mind stumbled away from the horror of that, and I suddenly remembered the photograph on the bedside table: a girl in the velvet drape, the curve of her throat, the bare shoulders. I had a physical sense of urgency — in my arms, in my breast — as though something vulnerable ought to be held close. I'd somehow shoved Vietnam far back in my mind. And yet Vietnam was the reason we were all there, in the burn ward, talking about a booby trap rigged with filth, talking about Pete, who was trapped now in the intensive care unit, the place they called the Cube with its machines and intravenous lines.

Dr. Caruso was outlining it carefully all over again: *Debridement* — which meant a cutting away of skin that would never heal. *Eschar* — what they called the ruined skin. I tried to picture the leathery burned skin giving way to the raw flesh underneath, and I missed part of what he said about preventing contractures of the elbows and fingers.

"Mrs. Duvall," Dr. Caruso said, as though he realized I'd lost my way. "Try to look after yourself. We don't want you keeping long vigils at Vincent's bedside. You've got to have a routine of your own."

In the window behind him, the sky was a cloudless square of blue. At home it would be even later in the day. At home it would have been time to put something together for supper.

Afterwards, as I passed the hubbub of the nurses' station and into the brightness of the first ward — all those boys smeared with Sulfamylon or wrapped in bandages — I remembered something Mary Kate said the morning Vincent left for Vietnam: *Nothing breaks that routine of yours, does it, Mom?* She was standing in the kitchen when she said it, looking at the jar of spaghetti sauce I had defrosting on the drain board.

Well, the routine was certainly broken now, I was thinking. I put a smile on, for there was Vincent, his chest smeared with Sulfamylon, his arms wrapped and splinted, his eyes all over the place again — panic or pain, or both.

I'd intended to tell him I was thinking of sticky buns, and to promise that the minute we got home I'd run down there and buy him a dozen. But instead I took my seat and said nothing at all.

Vincent said nothing either, at least not to me. His eyes were on the corpsmen hurrying back and forth. He addressed each one in the same high-pitched whine. "Help me back to bed. Hey — over here. Can you help me back to bed?" But it appeared they wanted him to sit up for awhile, and they kept putting him off.

7

When Vincent got his order for basic training in Ft. Benning, I took out the map of the United States so I could see exactly how far from Baltimore he'd be.

And after he was wounded, I took out the atlas in order to figure out why they flew him from Vietnam to Japan. I could see that it made sense — the evacuation hospital in Japan was the best place to match up the wounded soldiers with the people who had flown out from Texas to pick them up.

As for Vietnam, I'd seen the little maps in the newspaper. But it didn't help to study the map of Southeast Asia, because in that case it wasn't the distance that puzzled me. It was the reason.

And yet I couldn't allow myself to think whether or not the war was a just one. All along I'd been frightened, as any mother would be, but still I trusted that the President would do the right thing. *My country right or wrong*, Mary Kate once flung at me. I didn't know how to explain to her that it really wasn't a case of *my country right or wrong* if all along you believed your country *had* to be right, so therefore couldn't possibly do wrong.

Think Mom. They've got Vinnie now. I tried to think, but I also needed to keep moving, holding steady. I couldn't afford to entertain such a terrifying thought — that my own beloved country, the strong and valiant United States of America, might be careless with its boys.

I tried to keep moving, holding steady, but the problem was that when I got to the burn ward I was forced to sit. There was little I could actually do, little they'd allow me to do. Vincent was a soldier after all.

And so I had only the most basic of tasks to occupy me — getting food and drink to Vincent's mouth, tearing the sugar packets, cutting the meat, buttering the bread. But even those tasks could be taken from me in an instant. The occupational therapist, Lieutenant Darby, was forever patrolling the ward at mealtime. "Mrs. Duvall," he'd say, if I so much as propped a straw in Vincent's milk carton, "let's not do everything for him." I understood that Darby was only doing his job. I understood that the sooner Vincent achieved independence the better off he'd be. Still, more than any of the others, it was Lieutenant

Darby who made me wonder if I should have stayed out of the way, back at home.

One morning, down in the canteen, I picked up a magazine someone had left on the ledge and read an article about a pleasure boat that had capsized, throwing a man and his wife into the sea and trapping their little boy inside. It was one of those real-life dramas, with the terrified parents clinging helplessly to the hull until a fishing boat appeared miraculously on the scene. A young fisherman was strong enough to swim underneath, find the child, and pull him to safety. The photographs showed the smiling, muscular fisherman with an arm around the adorable child.

That story struck a chord with me. The parents, who had figured so prominently in the dramatic beginning, seemed to drift out of view once the rescuing fisherman was on the scene. The shift in focus made perfect sense. After all, what were the parents doing but hanging on helplessly? It wasn't really their story in the end.

I wasn't the only parent hanging on helplessly in the burn ward. There were the Muellers from Minnesota, whose son had been burned in a fuel tank explosion at Fort Sill, Maria Hernandez from Houston, whose son was just one month short of coming home from Vietnam when he was wounded, and Martha Jackson from New York, whose only child was burned so badly he was dying of the pain, which had caused a massive bleeding ulcer. I'd stop and chat with these other parents sometimes. They looked unmoored too. Some stayed a few days. Few stayed as long as I did.

There were many who never arrived at all. I could only suppose that they thought it best to do their waiting at home and stay out of the Army's way. Or maybe they didn't have the money for the trip, or maybe they were afraid.

Between the hours with Vincent, I walked all over the post. I even walked down to the historic Quadrangle, and joined the tourists inside the walls of the old fort, where tame deer lay in the shade of the taller trees, and a flock of regal peacocks paced on the lawn. I read the information plaques, and tried to work up some interest for Geronimo and Chief Natchez, Roosevelt's Rough Riders, General Pershing's campaign against Pancho Villa. But in truth I'd never been particularly interested in history, and the vacation atmosphere of the old fort got on my nerves — young parents with small children running around the lawn, everyone snapping pictures, the peacocks screaming and obligingly fanning their tails. The tourists didn't know about the other end of the post, where Vincent was being debrided in the tank. I could forgive them for their careless ease as they strolled about with their children in tow, but all the same I had to get away from them.

Eventually I established a routine of walking beyond the post gates and through the bordering neighborhoods. I got to know the face of each house along the way — this one with clipped hedges and tidy window boxes, that one with gaudy lawn ornaments and a sagging screen door. Did sadness lie behind the face of one house or the other? On Constance Avenue in Baltimore, the best-kept house on the block — white sheers at the two living room windows with the shades always drawn halfway, evenly, the pulls hanging like earrings — belonged to a couple whose child had died inexplicably in her crib only a couple of months after Jack was born. Over the years, every time I passed that house, I'd think about the lost child. *She'd be ten years old by now . . . She'd be a teenager, seventeen, old enough to go to the Junior prom.*

Sometimes I'd make a loop around a little park. It wasn't much more than a plot of grass dividing a boulevard, some sprawling live oaks, some swings and a rusting jungle gym. There were always two or three mothers at the fringe of the playground. They would look up from jiggling a baby carriage or pushing a stroller back and forth. They would smile at me, as though they recognized I was one of their own.

When Vincent was little, I'd take him out in the big old stroller I used to call the Cadillac — down Constance Avenue past the firehouse, because he loved the engines and sometimes the firemen would come out and make a fuss over him. And never could I have imagined back then that Vincent would be the child who would go off to war, and come home to a burn ward.

❍

Captain Garcia — the petite nurse with the pixie haircut, the one with the contagious laugh who was always kidding around with the corpsmen — stopped me on the way in. "You should know," she said matter-of-factly. "He's been having nightmares. Last night they had trouble settling him down. So he's a little rough around the edges this morning, Mom."

I thanked her for letting me know, but I would like to have shaken her. Nightmares now — as if the pain, and the debridement in the tank every single day, and Lieutenant Darby's mean exercise regimen weren't enough.

"Don't let it throw you," she said, picking up a chart and scribbling a quick note. "Nightmares aren't unusual. The mind has to work its way through the trauma too."

From off the ward — from the tank room — I heard a cry of pain. Surely she heard it too, but she didn't acknowledge it. She gave me a dismissive nod, and busied herself with her gown and a mask. When she opened the door to the Cube, I could hear the terrible sound of the respirators sighing.

Back on the ward, I found Vincent crying. Corporal Jenks had a hand on his shoulder, as though to keep him from leaping up to run away. When Vincent saw me, he opened his mouth and bawled loudly — not like he had bawled other times in pain, but like a cry of grief.

Corporal Jenks stepped back and gave me a grim smile. "Rough morning," he said.

"So I hear," I said.

"Mom?" Vincent cried.

"What is it, Sweetheart? I'm right here."

"He died, didn't he?"

"Who, Sweetheart?" I said steadily, and looked at Jenks, because I was afraid it was Pete who had died. Jenks frowned and shook his head.

"Brian," Vincent sobbed, "the pilot."

Brian. The name hit me like a punch to the chest. "Oh Vinnie," I said, " I didn't even know his name. Dr. Caruso did tell me. He said he died in Japan."

"He was so close, Mom," he said, looking not at me, but at his bandaged arms. "I could hear him." He turned his eyes to me. "So he never made it home?"

"No."

He looked around the ward, followed the entire progress of another corpsman maneuvering a cart piled with linens. "In Japan — I remember now," he said. "I think he was the one right beside me. Jesus." Tears spilled down his face, fell from his nose.

I took a tissue from my pocketbook.

He recoiled, as though I'd smacked him. "Please don't wipe my nose, Mom."

I froze, holding the tissue in my hand. What I really wanted to do was hold him in my arms. "Maybe I'd better leave you alone for a while," I said.

"No," he said softly. "Don't go."

So I sat down beside him again, my pocketbook on my lap, not daring to speak to a word.

"Take it easy, pal," Jenks said softly, and backed away.

Vincent closed his eyes. We sat like that, not even looking at each other, until another corpsman came with a thermometer. "How're we doing here?" he asked.

Vincent turned to me. "Maybe you better go now, Mom."

As I was leaving, I saw a girl standing outside the Cube, a tall girl in a yellow baby-doll dress, her hair teased up in a beehive — Pete's girl, the one in the photograph. Colonel Anderson was holding the surgical gown, while the girl slipped her arms in. From behind, another nurse quickly tied it at the neck and around the narrow waist. They gave her a mask. She tied the strings high on her head, in that dark pile of hair.

When they went into the Cube, I could see that the nurses were prepared for a scene when she looked around at the Cube, and saw that Pete had taken such a turn for the worse. Colonel Anderson had an arm around the girl's shoulder.

In the afternoon, Vincent was up in his chair. Lieutenant Darby was with him. Darby had a scrubbed look about him, like an altar boy. He nodded to me and returned his attentions to Vincent's elbows and the splints he'd made with his own strong and capable hands. I stood to the side while he kept making adjustments and fussing over the placement of the fingers. Vincent's whole body seemed to writhe slowly from the fixed points of those splints. Tears ran from his eyes.

But Darby kept talking about his car problems, about Three Dog Night coming to San Antonio, about riding his bike in the Hill Country. He talked mostly to Vincent, as though they were two Boy Scouts working on a science project and they'd just as soon ignore the mother in the room.

Vincent liked Lieutenant Darby, and called him Mike, which seemed odd to me, since Darby was an officer. "OK, Mike," Vincent would say, his teeth gritted against the pain. "Thanks, Mike."

"Mike's making me a special spoon," Vincent told me. "So I can feed myself."

After Darby packed up his things and left, I pulled a chair close to Vincent's and told him about seeing Pete's girlfriend. "Remember the picture he had on his bedside stand?"

"Yeah, I guess so."

It upset me to that he took little interest in this development. He'd always been such a sensitive boy, looking out for his friends. But now he seemed to have accepted Pete's disappearance into the Cube as a matter of course. It occurred to me that the pain had affected his ability to feel for others in the same way a burn affected the skin — like a thickening on the surface, a deadening.

He was shivering again, casting his eyes about in search of a corpsman to put him back to bed. It was no use trying to get through to him. Darby had wrung out everything he had to give. I went down to the canteen again, for yet another cup of coffee.

When I returned, there was a lot of activity around the bed that had been Pete's. They were moving in heat lamps, and moving out the wheelchairs and I.V. poles that had naturally accumulated in the vacant space. Either they were bringing Pete back, or they were preparing to move in someone new.

Vincent was drifting in and out of sleep. I sat quietly near the bottom of the bed, with my hand resting on his foot. I had gotten into the habit now of resting a hand on his foot, since I couldn't hold his hand.

"Have you heard anything about Pete?" I asked, when I saw him open his eyes.

"No." He closed his eyes again.

And so I went out to the nurses' station again, where Ann was writing on a chart.

"How's Pete Christie doing?" I asked.

She glanced at the Cube. "Very sick." She capped her pen, and clipped it to her pocket. "You're at the guesthouse, Mrs. Duvall?"

"Yes."

"Have you bumped into Caroline Brennan, Pete's girlfriend? She's at the guesthouse too."

"No. But I saw her on the ward. I know who she is."

She glanced at her watch, and turned away. "She's all alone," she said over her shoulder. "Maybe you could keep an eye out for her."

I was getting used to the abrupt turns the nurses could make. The pace on the burn ward was pitiless. The kindest people seemed to get caught and carried off in a breath. You'd be staring after them, left to fend for yourself. I watched the nurses, and I could divide them into two camps: the nurses who had been to Vietnam and the nurses who hadn't.

It was a good guess that a second lieutenant, like Ann Bukowsky, probably hadn't been to Vietnam, because anyone who had been over there for a year would have been promoted. But you had to look at the rest of them carefully, for there was more to it than age or rank. Some of them seemed to move with an ease that was heartbreaking to watch. It was though they had seen it all and nothing remained now to knock the wind from them. Those were surely the nurses who had been to Vietnam.

Captain Garcia, for example: Even if someone hadn't said so, I'd have guessed right off the bat that Captain Garcia was just back from Vietnam. I'd never thought about it before, but on the burn ward, with so much time to turn things over in my head, I saw it made sense: How else could a person work day after day on a burn ward if not by sealing off the heart with the awful work itself, if not by laughing and making jokes, all that bravado? I could only imagine the horrors those young people had to witness every day in the tank room, in the operating room, and when they were changing dressings — the horrors they protected me from, by sending me away. From a safe distance I had heard the crying. It had to have been terrible for them, to be the ones causing such pain.

And there was something else about Captain Garcia: She was a trained flight nurse, ready to drop everything and fly off with the doctors to Japan to pick up soldiers who had been evacuated. You could tell, just by the way the others deferred to her, that something more than rank set her apart.

As I was about to return to Vincent, the doors swung open. Pete's girlfriend, Caroline Brennan, was coming into the ward again. Colonel Anderson was with her, and the chaplain, Hal Trainer. There was no reason for me to stand there at the nurses' station, and yet I stayed until they put on their gowns, tied their masks, and passed into the Cube.

Then I hurried back to Vincent, and threw myself into talking about home: the Orioles and the Colts, Mary Kate and Jack, his friends, the boys he played ball with.

"Drink this, Vinnie," I kept saying. "Fluids will make you strong. We've got to get you well, so they'll let us take you home."

In all, a long day, and after dinner Lieutenant Darby appeared again, toting a special contraption for Vincent to try out, a spoon bolted to an angled handle. To me it looked jerrybuilt, like something out of a little boy's Erector Set. But somehow Darby managed to wedge it into Vincent's palm. With effort, Vincent bent his arm slightly and made the spoon dip toward the empty plate set up for the practice.

"Good," Darby said, when the spoon slid across a plate and rose again in the direction of Vincent's mouth. "Good job."

Tears ran down Vincent's cheeks.

"Good job," I said too.

"Don't be afraid to push that elbow," Darby said. "We got a ways to go there." He kept a firm hold on Vincent's splint and forced the elbow to bend.

Vincent writhed away from him. "Get off!" he screamed. "You goddamned son of a bitch!" The spoon contraption fell from his grip and hit the floor. Vincent gave it a kick and sent it spinning out into the room.

Lieutenant Darby was unperturbed. He kept a firm hold on the elbow.

"Get off! I hate you!" Vincent yelled.

Darby kept holding on. "You see this, soldier?" he said, nodding at the elbow, no emotion in his voice whatsoever.

Vincent blinked and looked at the elbow.

"You see the difference?" Darby said. "You just got yourself a couple inches of mobility. You keep working like that, and you'll be able to feed yourself. But I tell you what — You sit there on your ass, and you'll get contractures. It'll be like this elbow is sunk in cement. And your mom here can feed you for the rest of your life."

He let go of the elbow then, smiled at me polite as you please, and went to retrieve the spoon.

I felt a flash of hatred for Darby too, for the strong swing of his sun-tanned arm as he scooped up the spoon, for his cocky stride out of the ward.

All the color had drained from Vincent's face. "Just leave me alone, Mom," he said, as though I had taken some part in it.

I went back to the guesthouse, made a cup of tea in the kitchenette, and carried it into the dim parlor. Someone had left two empty beer bottles and a bag of pretzels on the table, but there wasn't another sign of life. Afterwards, I wandered out to the lobby, where the only thing to read was a post newspaper, nearly a week old. On the bulletin board I found the schedule for services on Sunday: *Roman Catholic Mass, Post Chapel, 0800 and 1100.*

Back in my room, I washed my hose in the sink, and laid out my church clothes: the navy blue linen, the white beads, the white straw hat with the cherries. I went to bed early, while it was still light out, because there was nothing else to do.

Later, when it was very dark, I woke up to a sound on the other side of the wall. Someone was crying, choking and sobbing — such a paralyzing sound I could only lie there, my heart in my throat. I got my rosary out from under the pillow and began to pray. Through the top slats of the blinds I could see three small lights shining steadily, the lights of Brooke Army Medical Center, where the night nurses were probably now making their rounds.

8

There's a holy card I've kept for many years between the pages of my missal, a picture of the Holy Family — the child Jesus playing in the foreground with a little toy horse, Joseph doing some carpentry off to the side, and Mary standing in the doorway to what appears to be the kitchen. Mary is blonde and pretty. She isn't looking at either Jesus or Joseph, but off into the distance, as though she's spotted something curious flying overhead. On the back of the card there's a prayer for a happy home. *Gentle Mary, meek and mild. . .*

One line stuck with me all the years I was raising children: *And Mary pondered these things in her heart. Pondered* seemed right to me. I liked that it had weight to it, implying a mother's heart, heavy with worry. *Pondered* didn't quite match up with *meek and mild*, or with the rosy, placid face of the Mary on the holy card.

○

The first Sunday in Fort Sam Houston, I was up and dressed early. I looked at myself in the mirror and wondered if Mary Kate had been right about the hat. The perky cherries on the band seemed almost inappropriate. But in the end I stuck with the familiar — a hat for Sunday Mass. I applied some lipstick. I took up my missal and pocketbook, brushed the lint from my dress, and set out for the Post Chapel.

Out on the main post road, distances were hard to judge. That post was flat as an ironing board. The day was heating up, and already I was perspiring in my hose. I thought of Mary Kate, and my sister Bonnie too, who were both perfectly comfortable going to church in bare legs.

Suddenly, I was startled by a short toot of a horn — Major Trainer in a small brown car. He came to a stop and leaned across to open the door.

"I assume you're going to Church," he said. "Come on, I'll give you a lift." He made room for me, dumping the books and papers from the front seat onto the floor in the back.

"How did you guess?" I asked, joking, because of course it was Sunday and I was carrying a missal in my hand.

"The hat," he said, and looked up at it.

He was wearing shorts and a sport shirt, which struck me as odd, for a man of the cloth on Sunday morning.

"Are you getting into a routine now?" he asked, pulling onto the road. "It's Kitty, isn't it? I hope you don't mind if I call you Kitty."

I told him Kitty would be fine, and that I was getting along all right. "At least on Sunday morning I know where to go and what to do," I said. "When I'm on the ward, I seem to get in the way."

"Oh, I rather doubt that," he said, raising his eyebrows. "Getting in the way isn't allowed up there. It might look like bedlam, but you've got Jeannette Anderson, and she runs a tight ship. Don't worry. If you're in the way, you'll be the first to know."

It made me laugh, to have that little worry snatched and tossed right out the open window. At the same time, something began to nag at me — the offhandedness with first names perhaps, not so much mine, because I was used to that with priests, but more with Colonel Anderson's. It was hard to place him. He didn't seem particularly military. Nor did he seem fatherly, like the parish priests I'd known, even the young ones. Hal Trainer — he said he preferred to be called Hal — would never address anyone as "my child." I tried not to look at his bare tanned legs. I couldn't remember the last time I'd sat alone in a car with a man other than Frank.

"I think you're doing fine," he said. "And it'll make a difference in Vincent's recovery." He flashed me a smile. "In case you're wondering, I'm on my way to play tennis."

I felt the color rush to my face. "It's a nice day for it."

"It's hot," he said, raising his eyebrows again. "But I like working up a sweat."

He switched on the radio, and one of those early Sunday morning programs came over the air, with the whiny organ struggling in the background and a small congregation singing unevenly up close. He fiddled with the dial and then it was Mexican music, wildly happy, strings and brass, singers calling *ie-yie* and clapping their hands.

We circled the big palm trees and came to a stop in front of a solid domed building. It reminded me of a municipal art museum.

"Here you go," he said, throwing his arm over the seat. "Fort Sam Houston Chapel." I got the impression he expected me to sit and chat for a while.

I thanked him and took up my missal and pocketbook.

"You're early," he said.

"That's all right," I said. "I'll have time to say some extra prayers."

"So say one for me, OK?" His tone was so casual, I wasn't sure he was serious. He was looking past me, in the direction of the chapel. "These days I think a lot about Job when I say my prayers," he added. "A place like the burn ward can do that, don't you think?"

I said yes, though I didn't know any more about Job than the old expression about his patience. He was smiling, waiting for me to say something more. I felt as though I'd made a wrong turn, right into a Protestant church, where Catholics weren't even supposed to sing along with the hymns. I thanked him again, and got out of the car.

"Hey, Kitty," he called through the window. "There's a bus you can take back. Look for the signs out on the main road. It'll be a hot walk."

The first thing I noticed about the Post Chapel was the carpeting, which made me homesick for St. Anthony's and the sound of my own steps on the marble approaching the altar. I picked a pew halfway to the front, and started in on my usual prayers.

It was an impressive chapel, with lots of carved wood and balconies going around, but the stained glass windows made me feel closed in — no pictures of Christ or the saints, just designs. There was no forgetting it was an Army Chapel either, not with all the colorful flags hanging on either side of the altar, and the people in uniform arriving.

I picked up the Bible in the pew, and flipped through until I found Job. I read idly, somewhere in the middle: *From the city the dying groan, and the throat of the wounded cries for help, yet God pays no attention to their prayer.*

I closed the Bible, and took out my rosary. It was actually a First Communion rosary that I'd found in the bottom of a dresser drawer, abandoned by one of the children years ago. As I held those little white beads in my fingers, it occurred to me that Vincent might very well have carried that rosary in the pocket of his white pants on his First Communion Day.

And then I was back to thinking about Vincent's terrible blanched fingers, and Lieutenant Darby forcing them to bend.

I kissed the crucifix and fell into the words of the *Memorare*. *O Mother of the Word Incarnate, despise not my petitions* — a favorite prayer that seemed to rise almost like a reflex whenever I was troubled. I pictured Mary bending down, holding out her arms. The *Memorare* had always been that sort of prayer to my way of thinking — a cry for Mother.

The priest and the altar boy arrived from the sacristy, and I felt then I was in the right place, opening my missal, giving myself over to the familiar words. I sang the hymns with all my heart: *O Lord I am not worthy that Thou shouldst come to me, but speak the words of comfort, my spirit healed shall be . . . Mother dearest, Mother fairest, help, O help, we cry to thee.* I closed my mind against the very idea of a God who pays no attention.

After Mass, emerging from the Chapel into the heat, I set out to find the bus stop. At an intersection on the main road I saw three military policemen, an older one and two young ones who seemed to be trainees. Their business was apparently nothing more than saluting the cars as they came and went. I called to them that I was looking for the bus to the hospital.

"Bamsey?" one of them called back.

I didn't know what Bamsey meant, but he was pointing down the road. "Here comes the bus now," he said. "You get on that, and it'll take you right to the door."

"To the hospital?" I called, just to be sure.

"Yes, ma'am. Bamsey."

The bus was nearly empty. I took a seat near the front by the window, and occupied myself with reading signs as they went by. TRA-DOC, with an arrow to the left, AMEDDC, CSM, BAMC with an arrow straight ahead. That's when I figured it out. *Bamsey* was BAMC — Brooke Army Medical Center, of course.

I got off at the guesthouse first, because I wanted to get out of my church clothes and put on something lighter. As I was coming in, I saw Pete's girlfriend sitting in the parlor, dressed in a flowered muumuu. The beehive had been dismantled, and her long dark hair lay in stiff bunches on her shoulders.

"You're Mrs. Duvall, aren't you?" she said. She didn't seem the least bit shy. "They told me to look you up. I'm Caroline Brennan. My boyfriend's on the burn ward with your son."

In a matter of minutes I had the whole story, which I'd thought would be about high school sweethearts, but was instead about a whirlwind romance that began in a bar in Austin, when Pete already had his orders for Vietnam. There was no mention of an engagement. She wasn't wearing a ring.

"I was down here a week ago and he looked great," she said. "But this time — " Her eyes filled with tears. "I really should go back tonight. My boss said I could take a couple days, but I don't know . . ."

I said the usual things — how the doctors were the very best, and how kind the nurses and corpsmen were.

"They are nice," she said, "especially Ann. She bought me a cup of coffee last week. That girl doesn't have it so easy herself." She took a pack of cigarettes from her pocket and offered me one.

I declined, and waited while she lit one and took a drag.

"She's got problems with her husband," she went on. "She told me he hasn't been right since he got back from Vietnam. They discharged him, but she has another year to go."

It wasn't surprising really. I'd sensed something from the moment I first saw Ann on the ward. The girl was so thin, so on guard.

"I bet he drinks too much," she said. "A lot of these guys do when they come back, you know." She paused, and squinted through the smoke. "I could be wrong about that. I mean, she never actually said he did. She seemed sorry she brought it up, actually. She changed the subject real quick when I started asking questions."

"I hope so," I said. "I mean I hope you're wrong about that."

She went to the window. "That's Pete's car out there. The Mustang convertible."

I went over to stand beside her. In the line of cars parked along the curb I saw a pale yellow convertible, the top down, the hood glinting in the sun.

"I was supposed to take care of it until he got back," she said. "Last week he had me drive up to the circle, and they wheeled him out so he could see it from the window."

"It's a nice car," I said, because what else was there to say to that? Beyond the yellow convertible, the post houses across the road, almost the same shade of yellow, seemed to puddle together in the glare. I allowed myself to picture that romantic ending — Pete recovered, coming down the front steps of Brooke Army Medical Center and slipping behind the wheel of his shiny yellow Mustang convertible, Caroline at his side.

"They said he might lose both his feet, you know," she said.

I was so stunned I could only stare into her pale face.

And then I had to hear her say it again. "They might have to amputate."

"I didn't know it was that bad," I said. *Things will look better in the morning*. I could see Pete winking at me. *Vince with the hands, and me with the feet.*

"It's bad," she said grimly. "Yesterday he was so sick he didn't even know who I was." She turned abruptly from the window and wiped her eyes fiercely on the back of her hand. "Listen — I'm going out and get something to eat. Off the post, I mean. You want to ride along?"

I had a clean tissue in my pocket, and handed it over. The whole time I'd been fighting the tears myself. "That would be nice," I said, "but how long do you think we'll be gone? I haven't been over to see Vincent yet."

She glanced at her watch. "We'll make it quick. Just give me a few minutes to get dressed."

I'd barely changed out of my church dress and hung it up when she appeared at the door, jingling her keys, in red shorts and a black skimpy top. Pale pink lipstick, the hair teased up again and anchored with a perky little scarf — the change was dramatic.

9

Vincent's guitar — I could picture the case under the eaves in the crawl space, between a box of Christmas ornaments and the Easter baskets, where I'd stored it after he left for basic training. But the odd thing was that I also remembered a letter he'd written from Vietnam, shortly after he got over there, in which he said he was learning a new song on the guitar.

What guitar had he been talking about? Had he bought another one in Vietnam, or had he borrowed one?

And what song had he learned? For a moment, before I caught myself, I thought I'd ask him about it. But how could we speak of guitars, when his hands were lying perfectly still on either side of that sherbet cup, his fingers swollen, white as marble?

❍

"Whoa!" Caroline said. "Hot." She turned on the ignition, and out of the radio came a screaming song about a honky-tonk woman. She settled a big pair of sunglasses onto her nose. "I don't know how you stand it. I think I'd go crazy if I were stuck here without a car."

It was the sort of thing only someone her age would say. At home in Baltimore, I was used to walking. There was only the one car, and I let my son Jack use it mostly, to get to work and to his classes at Loyola. I walked to work myself, and rode the number 3 bus when I wanted to shop downtown. On Saturdays I walked to the library and the bakery, and on Sundays to Mass at St. Anthony's.

"I don't mind," I said. "I have nowhere to go anyway. Just back and forth to the hospital."

We headed down the post road, cruising well above the speed limit, the heat rushing over our faces. I had the feeling that the handle on the car door wasn't enough, that I ought to grab hold of something more solid, that I was cruising far outside the limits of my own life. *Sunday morning,* I reminded myself. *It's still Sunday morning.* And I was heading away from the hospital, trapped now in a yellow convertible with a girl I hardly knew, and meanwhile Vincent would be looking for me, wondering.

We passed the officers' club and the big houses of the colonels and generals. At the gate we slowed down, and the military policeman waved us through. Caroline waved back, and he broke into a smile.

We passed the old Quadrangle, the iron fence, the stone compound, the deeper shade of the old trees.

"They keep deer in there," she said. "They're real tame, and you can walk right up to them. And peacocks too. I couldn't believe it."

"I know," I said. "I walked down here once."

"Good for you." She was looking straight ahead into her big sunglasses, and for a while we rode through the streets of San Antonio in silence. One good thing about riding in a convertible is the way the rush of air seems to excuse you from talking very much.

We rode up one block and down the other, through the shade of the taller city buildings and over the little stairways down to the river. Around the bend, old cypresses rose up from below the street. A tour boat passed slowly underneath them and out of view.

"Pretty nice, huh?" Caroline said. "Pete loves San Antonio. He took me to dinner on one of those boats the week before he left."

We entered a square with a small park at the center. A bell was ringing, and people were crossing in the direction of an old stone church. The color of the stones made it seem the face of the church was flooded with sunlight, though it was actually shaded by trees. Below all three arches, the dark wood doors stood open.

"San Fernando Cathedral," I said, reading the sign, and instinctively making the sign of the cross.

In some ways the scene seemed foreign — people dressed for church in cowboy boots and hats, others in bright Mexican fabrics. But the rest was so familiar — the bells, the young priest standing at the door in his embroidered white surplice. Inside, in the cool dimness, I knew there would be tiers of flickering votive candles, where the coins would clink atop the others in the metal box, where I could light two candles before the statue of the Blessed Mother, one for Vincent, another for Pete.

"Do you want to go in?" Caroline asked. "I can park and you can run in and take a look, if you want."

"It's eleven o'clock already," I said. "I don't think we have time." Besides, I couldn't very well just run in and take a look at a Mass.

We turned out of the square then, back the way we had just come, and shortly after pulled into the parking lot of a restaurant on Broadway

— Earl Abel's, the place Pete had mentioned.

"We can get something quick here," she said.

I followed her through the glassed-in lobby, passing several young families coming out, the children dressed up in Sunday clothes. It looked to be a very busy place, and I was worried it wouldn't be quick at all. But we were seated right away, and the waitress was sweet. "We'll get you set up in a jiffy," she said perkily.

I had to work at keeping up the conversation with Caroline. I asked about her job in Austin and she told me she worked for a couple of accountants.

"The younger one — Cliff — he's been so nice since this happened to Pete," she said. "He told me I could have more time off if I need it. But it's all so confusing. It's hard to know what to do."

"I know what you mean," I said, though I didn't really. It seemed perfectly clear to me what she ought to do — stay with Pete as long as she could.

Just after the waitress arrived with our plates, I noticed the three men being seated at the table opposite. I recognized one of them immediately: the burned man in the fedora, the one who had put me in the cab at the airport. I looked directly into his watery, red-rimmed eyes. He smiled and tipped his hat gallantly, but I wasn't certain he recognized me.

One of the other men at the table had been burned too. His hand was deformed and curled inward, stiff as a puppet's. He was a black man, and there was a sad contrast between his dark healthy skin and the shocking pink scars.

"I think I know that gentleman," I said quietly to Caroline, "the one in the hat. I met him in the airport."

She nodded. "I know him too. I met him up on the burn ward."

She seemed uncomfortable. She changed the subject, asking me about my other children.

I gave her a quick run-down on Jack and Mary Kate, and then I just naturally circled back to Vincent. "Vincent's the athlete in the family," I said. "He played basketball in high school. And he's the family musician too. He plays guitar, or I should say he tries to play the guitar."

She looked away. There was a clatter of dishes and silverware, the busboy clearing a table nearby. Within the noise, I realized what I'd just said. *He plays the guitar.* It was a reach for the familiar, only to feel the familiar break.

Caroline took out her wallet. I offered to pay, but she wouldn't let me. When she stood up, the men at the table looked over and waved.

"Hey, Caroline," the one in the fedora said. "Remember me? Will Bishop, from up on 14A?"

She smiled blindly in the direction of his table. "Yes," she said. "I think so."

"Who can forget a face like this?" he said, and the other men laughed.

She maintained the smile, but didn't laugh.

"Sorry," he said. "That's just a little of our crispy critter humor. How's Pete doing?"

"Not so good. They had to put him in intensive care."

"In the Cube? Gee, I'm sorry to hear that."

The one with the burned hands shook his head and said he was sorry too. The other one, with the brace on his elbow, murmured "Shit."

"You tell him we said Hi," Will said. "Tell him we said go the extra mile."

She nodded, waved the bill like a lace handkerchief, and headed for the cashier.

"Do you remember me, Will?" I asked. "You got me a cab at the airport."

He frowned. "Hey, I do remember. Small world."

I asked if he'd met Vincent. He said he didn't think so. I looked at the other two, but they shook their heads.

"So how's your son doing?" Will asked.

"He's coming along," I said. "It's hard, of course."

"Damn straight. What per cent is he?"

"Thirty-six." How strange to have the number handy, like a special classification badge for Vincent.

"Maybe I'll get to meet him. Us crispy critters have to stick together."

"Yeah," the black man said. "And we like to keep an eye on those mad docs."

"And Hal Trainer," the other one said. "The wild preacher man. Is he still assigned up there?"

"He is," I said, and laughed. "Would you like me to tell him you said hello?"

"Tell him you bumped into the Crispy Critter Club down at the Earl Abel's," Will said. "He'll know who we are."

Caroline had already paid the bill and was waiting for me up by the cashier.

"It was nice to meet you all," I said. "Don't forget to look for my son if you come up to the burn ward — Vincent Duvall."

Afterwards, out in the car, I smiled across at Caroline. "Well that was certainly interesting," I said.

"Yes." She had her eye on the road. "Very."

I rambled on about the coincidence — meeting a burn patient in the airport, and then bumping into him again in a restaurant, and come to find out he knew Pete.

"Well, if you think about it," she said, "it's not such a coincidence really. They send all their burn patients here. Some of them hang around, like those guys. There are probably more burned soldiers in this city than anywhere else in the country."

She turned up the radio then — Elvis crooning "Suspicious Minds."

I made a little small talk about the climate in San Antonio versus the climate in Baltimore and Austin. But then I gave it up, and we rode the rest of the way without talking much, the hot air blowing over our faces, all the way back to the circle in front of the hospital.

"Door to door service," I said. "Thank you."

"You're welcome. Maybe I'll see you next time."

When I got to the top of the hospital steps, I looked back. The yellow convertible was picking up speed, heading back to the guesthouse, but just as likely heading for Austin soon after.

Up on the ward, Vincent was with Father Smith, a tall, round-shouldered young man who was prematurely bald.

"And here's your mother," Father Smith said, finishing the sign of the cross crisply, looking up to smile at me. Vincent opened his eyes long enough to take me in, then closed them again.

Father Smith stepped back from the bedside. "I brought him communion," he whispered, taking my hand in his cool, damp grasp.

"Thank you, Father," I said. *Sunday. Communion.* I was still standing firmly in ordinary time.

10

A woman's work is never done. Truth is, there was something about housework I really liked, back then. There was more to it than washing dishes and vacuuming and doing the laundry. To my way of thinking, a woman's work was never done because there was more to keeping house than housework. A big cleaning in both spring and fall, in particular the washing of the windows, had to do with something deeper than dust and grit. I'd hose off the screens, and wash the glass with ammonia and wads of newspaper. I'd hang the dark green shades, take down the heavy draperies — the lined brocades that had once belonged to my Aunt Claudette — and air them on the line. After the sheers had been washed and ironed, and the little rips in the hem mended, I'd shirr them on the rod at the shining window. And then a buoyant feeling would come over me, hard to describe. It had to do with some sort of connection I was keeping — time passing, and yet the house around me, and around my children, holding beautifully still.

There is a singular moment that my mind returns to every now and then, a spring afternoon when I'd just finished washing the downstairs windows and hanging the curtains. Suddenly the children came bursting into the house from the back yard, and I saw how they stopped at the edge of the dining room rug, looking about them, taking it in. What did children care about the cleaning up of dirt? It was the move forward into a new season they'd noticed. The light and color of it, the dear smell of it, blowing through the screens still wet from the scrubbing.

Woman's work was something I was taught, by my mother and my grandmother. But it was unlikely I'd pass that on to my daughter Mary Kate. Mary Kate would have a conniption at the very idea, would brush it off before I could ever find the words to explain.

❍

Vincent had been in the tank room longer than usual, and I didn't know whether to wait or to go back the guesthouse. The whole ward seemed to be out of kilter. I pushed my chair into the corner by the bedside stand and tried to be inconspicuous. Captain Garcia was bristling about, towing two fresh-faced corpsmen who kept giving each other bewildered looks behind her back.

Captain Garcia shot a look in my direction.

"I was waiting to see Dr. Caruso," I said.

"Rounds have already been through," she said sharply. "You probably won't catch him until this afternoon."

Another corpsman arrived, looking for Vincent. "I'm supposed to bring him back to Colonel Beck for spirometry," he said to Captain Garcia.

"Spirometry?" I asked.

"It's Colonel Beck's research project," she said. "Don't get yourself into an uproar. He's doing everybody on the ward."

I wandered out to the nurses' station then, where Colonel Anderson was talking to several officers in Air Force uniforms, giving them the tour. The door was standing open, and I could see Pete. Except for the intravenous bottles hanging above, and the bag of ominously dark urine, he seemed misplaced among the others, whose burns appeared more catastrophic. The lower half of his body — the burned half — was entirely hidden by the sheets falling in perfect pleats from the over-bed frame. It appeared he was just sleeping, peacefully.

Later I saw Colonel Anderson coming back from the elevator. It wasn't really my business, but it seemed I'd left those polite ways behind in Baltimore. I went to her and asked outright if it was true that Pete was going to lose his feet.

She smiled wanly at me. "We hope not, Mrs. Duvall."

"Are his parents coming?"

"There's only a mother, and apparently she's unable to travel. She's been ill, a fragile diabetic." She sighed, shaking her head. "His girlfriend was here earlier — Caroline."

"She's left already," I blurted out. "I wish she'd stayed with him."

"Oh, Mrs. Duvall," she said. "You have to understand how it is for these girls, the sweethearts and even the new brides. They fly in here so excited about their young men coming home, and then they get hit with all of this. Sometimes they just have to bail out."

After she went into the ward, I saw Hal Trainer coming down the corridor, whistling and waving to one of the corpsmen. I stood by the nurses' station while he pulled a gown over his uniform.

"Everything all right?" he asked me, lifting the mask to his face.

I shook my head. "I was just asking about Pete."

"You want to go in with me to say hello?" he asked, and lowered the mask from his face.

I hesitated. And meanwhile Captain Garcia arrived from around the corner.

"All right if I take Mrs. Duvall into the Cube with me?" Hal asked her. "To say hello to Lieutenant Christie?"

She raised her eyebrows. "It's all right with me. But keep it short, Padre."

He winked. "Yes ma'am." He pulled a gown from the cart and handed it to me. "You have to put on a clean gown," he said, and waited at the door to the Cube, joking around with the one of the doctors who happened to come out, teasing him about his tennis game.

When I was all set in gown and mask, he tied his mask on too. "After you," he said.

I passed before him into the wheezing sound of respirators. I took a place at one side of Pete's bed, and he went around to the other.

I knew at once that Pete wouldn't open his eyes, and wondered why they had bothered to secure the oxygen tube to his pillow, for it looked as though he was not about to move ever again. Someone had dampened his hair and parted it sharply like a little boy's, the way a mother would before church on Sunday.

"Look who's stopped by to say hello, Pete," Hal said, folding Pete's fingers into his square brown hand, taking care with the intravenous lines. "It's Kitty Duvall — Vincent's mother. You remember her, don't you?" He looked across at me, his gaze intense above the mask.

"Hello Pete," I said. "Vincent really misses you. You get better, OK?"

There was no sound, only the faint whistling of the oxygen.

"That's all right, Pete," Hal said. "You just conserve the fighting strength. We'll talk, and you listen for a change." He talked casually, about everyday things — the Texas Longhorns, a small tornado touching down west of the city, and how he had beat Major Wallace at tennis. "You know Major Wallace, don't you, Pete?" He leaned closer to Pete's ear. "Don't tell him I said this, but he's really out of shape."

Two doctors arrived at Pete's bed. One stood at the foot, writing on a chart. The other excused himself, stepped in front of Hal, and bent down to look at the urine in the bag.

"How are we doing here today?" he asked no one in particular.

"Looks like we're worn out," Hal said.

"Pete," the doctor said, squinting at the intravenous line, and reaching out to adjust the drip. "It's Colonel Tribble. How's it going?"

There was no response. The doctors moved on.

Hal leaned close to Pete again. "Before I go, I'd like to pray. I hope that's OK with you." He took Pete's hand in his, and looked at me. I understood, and took Pete's other hand, folding his dry, limp fingers in my own.

"Lord," he began, "Pete and Kitty and I are calling your name. Help us feel your healing presence."

I hardly heard the rest, and yet, halfway through, I felt I'd been taken up, not by any particular words, but by the effort of it, in the face of what seemed such awful forsakenness.

On the other side of the Cube, a corpsman turned on the suction machine. Encircled by tubes and intravenous lines lay a boy slathered with Sulfamylon, naked but for the washcloth someone had placed carefully over his the privates, the way Jesus is always covered on a crucifix. There was no face left to pity, only the swollen shape of a face, and the tube running from his mouth to the machine. If that boy had wanted to cry, how could he have made a sound?

I looked at Hal — his eyes closed, his head bent. I was thinking of the line from Job, about the throat of the wounded crying for help, and wondered if that was what the Book of Job was all about in the end — That even though it seems God isn't paying attention, someone continues to pray.

And then I heard Hal speak softly a line I have carried in my heart ever since: "When you walk though fire you shall not be burned. You are precious in my eyes. Fear not, I am with you."

When we were outside the Cube, Hal thanked me. "This sort of thing makes a difference," he said, stripping off his gown. "We have to assume he heard us."

He followed me to the ward, but Vincent still wasn't back from the tank room.

"It's going to be a while, Mom," Captain Garcia said wearily.

"He's all right, isn't he?" I asked.

"He's fine. Go get yourself a cup of coffee or something. Stop worrying."

"Come on," Hal said. "I'm buying. I could use a cup myself."

We went down to the canteen and sat at a table in the corner. People would come in to buy a cup of coffee, or cigarettes from the machine, but no one actually sat down.

"So, was the Post Chapel to your liking?" Hal asked, smiling slyly, as though he already knew the answer.

"Well, it's carpeted," I said right off the bat.

He threw his head back and laughed. "Of course you'd notice that. You've got that old Catholic craving for marble."

I laughed too. "But a Mass is a Mass. I guess something like that shouldn't matter."

"Oh, but it does matter."

I looked at my nearly empty cup and wished I had another, if only to keep the conversation going. It was so pleasant, to just sit and talk.

"It's a very historical Chapel, you know," he went on. "Hey, I know a place you have to see. The Cathedral — San Fernando. You shouldn't miss that."

"Actually, I saw it the other day," I said, and went on to tell him about Caroline and the ride in Pete's convertible, Earl Abel's, and meeting Will Bishop and his friends — such a coincidence, after meeting him in the airport.

He smiled and shook his head. "Will Bishop. What a crazy guy."

"He said the same about you."

He laughed. "I think he's under the impression that he broke me into the burn ward." He went on to say that Will was from Rhode Island, that he came back regularly to visit the burn ward, and had even rented a place off-post. Apparently money wasn't a problem, because his father was well off.

"I like Will," I said. "I was hoping Vincent would meet him."

I chattered on, branching into side stories, moving backwards — the taxi driver and his nephew Carlos, my first ride in an airplane, arriving at Fort Sam Houston by taxi. I even remembered to ask him about the Latin motto above the door of the hospital.

"Let's see," he said. "Roughly translated, I believe it says 'Not for oneself, but for others, giving health to mankind.'" He raised his eyebrows. "You certainly have an eye for detail."

"It can be a burden," I said, "like carrying around too much stuff in your pocketbook. But I guess you think I've completely forgot about Vincent. I haven't mentioned him once since we sat down."

"I know all about what's going on with Vincent," he said. "But I wouldn't want to have missed the Mustang convertible story."

"I wish I'd been more help to that poor girl," I said. "I wanted to tell her everything would be all right, but it seemed such an empty thing to say."

It was unnerving to look directly at him. He was looking right at me, as though every word were worth his consideration. When he leaned forward on the table, I had to glance away, at the little cross on his lapel. I felt the warmth in my face, and wondered if he'd noticed.

"It doesn't sound empty to me," he said, "because you mean it. Everything will be all right — because you have your faith. At least I think that's what you mean."

I nodded. But in truth, if I'd told that girl everything would be all right, it would mostly have been to convince her to stay there with Pete.

"Like the psalmist says," he said, "though we walk through the valley of the shadow of death, everything will be all right."

That wasn't the way I remembered the psalm, but there was nothing in his face that said he was being sarcastic. He picked up the saltshaker, and stood it between us, as though he were about to illustrate a point. Then he moved it back to where it was before. "As for Caroline, it could be she can't accept any of this as all right," he said. "Maybe she's got a picture in her mind of how things ought to be, and she can't let it go."

What came to mind was that picture of Caroline herself, the one Pete used to have on his bedside stand. I wondered what the corpsmen had done with it. There was certainly no room in the Cube for a photograph in a fancy frame. *Fiancé.* I could hear Pete saying it. That was his picture of how things ought to be, a picture it seemed he had let go, without realizing it, while he lay with his eyes closed, drifting off into a terrible fever and a nightmare about a booby trap.

"Say," he said, "not to change the subject, but have you heard about the famous Brooke Army Medical Center Peace Symbol?"

He seemed pleased that I hadn't, and he shifted his chair so he could lean against the wall. "Have you noticed that the parking lot in front of the hospital is perfectly circular? And then there're these sidewalks crossing it?"

"I can't say that I have."

"Well, have a look the next time you're out there. Those sidewalks used to be footpaths, just dead grass where people would cut across. But of course the Army couldn't abide such untidiness, and they had to pave them over." He laced his hands behind his head, taking his time with the punch line.

"So I guess they ended up with something in the shape of a peace symbol?" I said, playing along.

"Bingo. A great big peace symbol in concrete."

"Oh my."

He laughed, and went on to say that they still kept a suite for LBJ upstairs, because his ranch was only about fifty miles up the road, in the Hill Country. They flew him in once in a while so the doctors could look after him. "Apparently nobody has a better view of the Brooke Army Medical Center peace symbol than LBJ does," he said.

"I should tell that one to my daughter Mary Kate," I said. "She's got peace symbols stuck all over her car."

"But you haven't heard it all. Now it seems they're drawing up plans to put in new sidewalks — to break the symbol, so to speak."

"An even better story for Mary Kate."

"So your daughter's in the peace movement?"

"Yes indeed. I'm afraid she'll get arrested one of these days."

"And how about you?" he asked, with a crooked smile. "Any peace symbols stuck to your car?"

"There's nothing on my car but dirt."

"So," he said, "What do you think about the war, if you don't mind my asking?"

I didn't mind him asking, but I didn't know how to answer either. It had never really been clear to me why President Johnson had sent the troops in the first place, or why he kept sending them, and now it was President Nixon sending them. I sometimes saw myself as Mary Kate must have seen me — blinking dumbly in the face of her anti-war outbursts, carrying dishes back and forth to kitchen, leaving the heated politics at the table. "I guess I'm just confused," I said.

"Who wouldn't be confused?" he said matter-of-factly. "And your other son — Does he take part in the protests too?"

"No. Jack isn't one to rock the boat."

It occurred to me that this chaplain might be married and have children, maybe even a child who tried his patience or caused him heartache and worry. He didn't wear a wedding band, but then a lot of men didn't wear them. But I couldn't very well ask.

When we parted in the lobby, he winked at me. "Goodbye, Kitty Duvall," he said, as though my name gave him particular pleasure.

11

In sickness and in health.

I tried to explain to each of the children — when they were old enough to understand — that their father couldn't help drinking, that it was a sickness really.

So many times I stood at the window, long after they were in bed, watching and praying that their father wasn't drunk behind the wheel, that he wouldn't cause some terrible accident. A prayer would rise from me in the dark — a wordless prayer, a silent cry. I felt so alone, abandoned.

One year Frank had to spend a month in the state hospital, drying out. When the month was up, I drove out there to pick him up. He had already checked out when I arrived, and was waiting for me at the curb.

I'd gotten all dressed up for the occasion. I was so relieved to have him coming home. But my nervous chattering must have unnerved him, because he hunkered down immediately against the passenger door, as though at any moment he might leap out and tear down the road.

"You're a hard person to live with, Kitty," he said, out of the blue.

I actually laughed. Frank was the alcoholic, and who could be harder to live with than an alcoholic? But he didn't crack a smile, didn't even turn to look at me.

We were approaching the hospital gate, passing the last of the cottages where the patients were housed. To the right was a little wooded area, so pretty with the azaleas in bloom. Back home, the children were waiting for us, at their Aunt Bonnie's house.

"Aren't you happy to be going home?" I asked.

"Is that what you want me to say?" He wouldn't even turn his face from the window. "That I'm happy?"

"You'll feel better, Frank," I said. "It's going to be all right."

All along I'd been telling myself that he couldn't do the right thing for me and for the children because he was sick, because of the drinking. But that day it struck me it might actually be the other way around: Maybe he never did have it in him to stay with us, but all the same he was trapped, and being trapped was driving him to drink.

So maybe it would have been a kindness then, to set him free, to say, "I've had enough, Frank — Just go." But that was something I never did have in me. So I just hung on, praying he'd get better, and meanwhile he kept pulling away, until finally the connection between us snapped.

❍

"How about we take a little stroll?" Hal said to Vincent.

Vincent shrugged, as though he couldn't care less.

"Why don't you come along too?" Hal said to me. "Maybe we'll go off the ward a little ways. What do you say, Vincent? I'm buying the drinks."

"OK," Vincent said, getting to his feet, sliding into his slippers, "if you think they'll let me."

We asked Captain Garcia, and she said it would be all right. "But let's get you decent first," she said. "You're a little exposed in the back." She got Vincent a bathrobe from the linen cupboard. She draped it over his shoulders and gave him a little pat. "Nice and steady with him, Padre," she said to Hal.

We walked as far as the waiting room. Vincent sat down on the sofa by the window, in the exact spot where I'd been sitting so much of late. Strange, what a thrill it gave me to see him sitting there.

"I'll be right back," Hal said, and returned a few minutes later, juggling three paper cups with small, sloppy scoops of ice cream floating on top. "Root beer floats," he said. He handed one to me and placed Vincent's within reach on the end table. He dealt out three plastic spoons, and stuck a straw in each cup.

The last time I'd had a root beer float was probably before the children were born. I took a sip, and regretted instantly that it was so small.

"So," Hal said, looking at Vincent. "You're making big progress. What will you do with yourself when you go home to Baltimore?"

Vincent sucked on the straw and looked sidelong at him. "I don't know yet."

"What about college? You'll get the G.I. Bill."

"Maybe later, when I figure out what I want."

"Well, just so you eventually do the figuring. How about music? You play the guitar, right? You could study music."

"The guitar was mostly for fun." He took a breath, and sat up straighter in the chair. "Maybe I'd like to do what Mike Darby does."

Hal nodded thoughtfully. "Occupational therapy."

"Yeah. But I guess you need really strong hands for that kind of work."

"Well, you need to be strong, that's for sure. But I don't know that the hands are the most important. You could do it, if you really put your mind to it."

Hal glanced at me, but I thought it best to hold my tongue. Motherly advice had never held much sway with Vincent.

Vincent loudly sucked up the last of the root beer and peered at the ice cream left in the bottom of the cup.

"Allow me," Hal said, and fed him the ice cream in two bites.

"I ought to get back," Vincent said, getting to his feet. It was the first time I'd seen him get to his feet without being told to since before he was burned.

"Yeah. Me too," Hal said, standing up, smiling down at me. "So we'll see you later, Kitty?"

"Yes," I said.

Vincent was already walking away, bent over with the effort. I saw that the sash to his robe was loose and sweeping the floor, but I let it be.

That afternoon there were two pieces of mail for Vincent, both of them re-routed from Vietnam — a card I'd mailed weeks earlier, and a letter with the return address of "B. Houck," at the Mercy Nurses' Residence on Pleasant Street, Baltimore.

Barbara Houck was the girl who had invited Vincent to the prom at Catholic High. I'd never met her, but remembered Vincent showing me a photograph of a pretty girl in a pale blue prom gown.

I found Vincent up in the chair, trembling with a chill. They had glued little hooks to his fingernails, and rigged up ten tension lines anchored at the elbow. The corpsman explained that it was to keep Vincent's fingers from curling in. My first thought was that the hooks looked exactly like the hooks on the Coats and Clark card in my sewing box at home — little black hooks suitable for the waistband of a dark-colored skirt. My second thought was that the tension lines looked like strings on guitar.

"Mail for you," I said, as cheerfully as I could, and opened the one from me first. It was a card I'd bought in the Rexall drugstore, a silly thing with a moping hound dog on the front, and *Missing you* inside. I'd mailed it more than a month earlier, and had written only a couple of lines inside about the Fourth of July parade in Towson.

Then I opened the letter from Barbara and spread it out for him to read — curly peacock-blue ink on pale blue stationery, writing on both sides. While he read, I pretended to be sorting out papers in my pocketbook. He asked me to flip the page over for him, and I couldn't help but notice the prominent x's and o's on the back.

"You can put this in the drawer," he said, when he was finished. "It's from Barb Houck. She mailed it a long time ago. And anyway, I just talked to her on the phone."

"What phone?" It was news to me he could talk on the phone.

"Out by the desk. Mike helped me."

"Well, that's nice, honey. This is the girl you went to the prom with? When did she call?"

"I called her." He smiled sheepishly. "I couldn't believe she was there. She's always on duty. She's in nursing school, you know."

Before I could get any details, Dr. Caruso arrived with a corpsman in tow. The corpsman set up a surgical tray, and gave me quick look, like he thought I ought to leave.

"Why don't you stay, Mrs. Duvall," Dr. Caruso said. "This will only take a minute. I just want a look."

He put on his gloves, carefully pulled the dressing away from Vincent's forearm, and I could see the pieces of animal skins, scraps of hide in different shades of gray, or gray with white spots. There was something bizarrely reassuring about the way they had been pieced so carefully, edge to irregular edge, like a crazy-quilt over Vincent's raw flesh.

"What you're seeing here is pig skin," Dr. Caruso said, not looking at me but at his handwork. "It's temporary. Tomorrow, if we have any, we might apply homografts."

He explained that a homograft is human skin, donated by someone who has died. Homografts were temporary measures too. All of it would be temporary until they could graft Vincent's own skin. This they called an autograft.

I took a look at the pig skin that was still in the little dish on the surgical tray. I was wondering what the skin of a human being would look like — the skin of some young soldier who had died, someone else's child?

Dr. Caruso used the tweezers to lift one of the pig skin patches from the wrist, and Vincent winced.

"See how these are beginning to adhere?" Dr. Caruso said. "That's a good sign. Granulation tissue."

Granulation: I was picturing granulated sugar, of course, but didn't ask him how the terms connected.

I was learning to read the pattern of the damage. The burns on Vincent's chest and shoulders — the areas covered with Sulfamylon — were gradually healing on their own. But some of the skin on his arms and hands wouldn't ever heal on its own, and had to be cut away. That was the ugly-sounding *eschar*, the bad skin that could never be good again. Other skins — pig skin, dog skin, the skin of human cadavers — would cover the wounds for a while.

Eventually Dr. Caruso would have to take some of Vincent's own healthy, unburned skin from the legs, and then there would be brand new wound that would have to heal. To me it seemed like robbing Peter to pay Paul, but Dr. Caruso explained that he would only take a partial layer of skin from the donor site, that it would be able to heal cleanly in time, whereas the badly burned areas would not.

It was one thing to hear the explanation, but it was another to actually see that fuzzy skin of a gray and white pig, pieced against the back of your own son's hand.

Dr. Caruso replaced the dressing meticulously, snapped the gloves from his hands, and finally looked me in the eye. "I'm scheduled for the next flight to Japan," he said, with his customary careful smile. "We'll do the autografts as soon as I get back."

"You have to go to Japan?" I didn't even try to hide my dismay.

"We have troops to bring back, Mrs. Duvall," he said. "Dr. Nuttell will take over in the mean time. You'll be in good hands."

I liked Dr. Nuttell. He was a heavy-set, balding fellow who reminded me of my brother-in-law Richard. He was more outgoing than Dr. Caruso, and would sometimes stop at Vincent's bed for no other reason than to tell a "knock, knock" joke. I knew he was a smart doctor. All of them assigned to the burn unit were smart, probably hand-picked out of the best. But none of that mattered, because it didn't seem fair they would snatch Dr. Caruso away from Vincent, and put him on a plane bound for Japan, so many miles over all that sea.

"But what about the homografts?" I'd never spoken the word before, and stumbled over the pronunciation. *Homo*-graft: skin taken from a human being, not from a pig or a dog.

"Dr. Nuttell can apply them," he said. "It not a big deal."

It seemed to me that a homograft ought to be a very big deal indeed. "I'll be worried about you," I said.

"About me?" He gave a short laugh. "Don't worry. They take good care of us. I'll be back before you know it."

After he left, I was tired and discouraged. I told Vincent I was going back to my room for a rest.

"Before you go," he said, "would you hand me that letter again?"

I spread the letter out for him on the tray, and when I looked back at him from the door, he was bent forward with his splinted arms framing that single sheet of dainty blue paper. Beyond him, in the second ward, someone was crying in pain — a constant, writhing *Oh, Oh, Oh.* I realized that the crying had been going on for a while, that I hadn't paid it any mind. I wondered if I might be getting used to those cries, or learning in some horrifying way to tune them out.

Downstairs, I saw Ann Bukowsky coming in, hurrying up the front steps. Beyond her, in the circle, a white car idled at the curb — a battered-looking car, with a stripe of rust along in the side. The man at the wheel was leaning across the seat, watching after Ann.

I called hello to Ann, but she barely waved back. When I passed the white car, I glanced at the driver. He was a bony young man with wild hair and a straggly mustache. He wasn't wearing a shirt, which shouldn't have seemed odd, given the heat, and yet in that particular place — in front of Brooke Army Medical Center, where just about everyone hurrying in or hurrying out wore a creased uniform and a perfectly-positioned hat — it struck me as odd.

I remembered what Caroline said. *I bet he drinks too much.* And maybe he took drugs too, I was thinking. It wasn't the long hair and the way he was dressed that said so, but something I couldn't put a finger on, something unsettling in the way he was still staring after Ann, though she was already out of sight.

I walked slowly back to the guesthouse, because it was hot, and because I was so tired. I kept thinking about the past two days, and the pattern in it: Caroline and Pete, a girl named Barbara writing to Vincent, a yellow convertible, a letter on blue paper. The more I thought about it, the further the pattern extended, deepening, turning darker, taking in Ann Bukowsky and her husband too.

I could still see that yellow convertible turning out of the hospital circle and heading back to Austin. And I remembered what Colonel Anderson said: *Sometimes they just have to bail out*. How hard would it be for Vincent, to be dumped by a girlfriend — that pretty girl in the blue prom dress — because she couldn't deal with those awful burned hands?

That very afternoon the pay phone rang in the hall outside my room and I was surprised by a call from Mary Kate.

"Wait 'til you hear this, Mom," she said. "Vinnie's little girlfriend is flying down to see him. Barbara Houck — Remember her?"

"I remember," I said. "But what do you mean she's coming here?"

"Well apparently she and Vinnie were writing to each other the whole time he was in Vietnam. Sounds kind of serious." She laughed girlishly. "And so she wants to see him."

"How do you know this?" I asked.

"She called yesterday. Jack gave her my number. Her brother and Jack were in the same class."

"This isn't such a good idea, Mary Kate," I said. "You've got to call her back and persuade her to wait a little while."

"But Vinnie asked her to come," she said, as though that settled everything. "Besides, it sounds like she's got her mind made up. She already asked the nuns for a couple days off — She's in nursing school at Mercy Hospital, you know." She interrupted herself then and said something I didn't catch, something about the news on TV, which I could hear in the background.

I waited, and then she was back, going on about Nixon, how he had promised to pull out the troops and now was doing the opposite. "Who does that guy think he's fooling?" she asked.

"I don't have much time for the news," I said. "I've got other things on my mind."

She shifted gears then, and asked me about the skin grafts. Would they do them on the burn ward, or would then send him to the V.A. for that?

"The V.A.?"

"The Veteran's hospital."

That was the problem with Mary Kate on the phone — all the questions, not just the ones I couldn't answer, but also the ones I'd never have thought to ask. "For heaven's sake," I said. "No one's even mentioned the V.A. We're taking it a day at a time here."

"Relax, Mom," she said, and launched the subject of coming down to see Vincent herself — and Jack coming too — and did I think they ought to spread the visits out or come together?

All of this worried me, because I didn't know how we would afford airfare for both Mary Kate and Jack, and I was suddenly afraid of plane crashes, and most of all I just couldn't imagine how — once they were safe on the ground in San Antonio — I'd ever manage to usher the two of them onto the burn ward.

But Mary Kate seemed to have all that figured out. "Don't worry," she said, just before we hung up.

I considered calling Barbara Houck's mother, as if there were some sort of problem at school that the mothers could handle over the telephone. But in the end I put the call in to Barbara herself, at the Mercy nurses' residence.

The woman who answered was probably a housemother, and when I told her I was calling long distance from Texas she said, "Hold on, Hon — I just saw Miss Houck come in, so I know she's here." She put me through to the floor, and a girl answered on the first ring. When the housemother told her to run down to Miss Houck's room quick because there was a call from Texas, I could hear the screeching down the hall. "Barb, Barb! It's for you. It's Vinnie!"

When Barbara picked up, her hello was breathless and happy.

"Barbara, this is Kitty Duvall, Vincent's mother," I said. "Don't worry — Everything's all right."

"Oh!" she said. "Thank God."

I immediately lost track of what I'd planned to say. "How are you?" I asked stupidly.

"I'm just fine, Mrs. Duvall. But how are you? It must be terrible for you. And all alone down there."

"Well, I'm not really alone," I said quickly. "They give the family plenty of support. They're very supportive." And then I plunged right in: "Mary Kate tells me you're thinking of coming down."

"It's all right, isn't it?" she said. "With you, I mean?"

"Well, of course it's all right with me. It's just that Vincent's condition is really touch and go. Maybe he sounds fine on the telephone, but he's confused sometimes — "

She cut in. "You don't have to worry about me. I'm in nursing school now, and I'm not scared of burns, really I'm not. I want to see him in the worst way, and actually he asked me to come. Besides, I've already got my ticket."

She was to arrive in two days, in the evening, and I wasn't to worry about a thing, not even about meeting her at the airport. Everything had been arranged. She just needed to know if it was really as hot as they said it was in San Antonio, and what sort of clothes she ought to pack.

The operator interrupted, and I had to deposit more coins.

"Oh my god," Barbara said. "I'm blabbing away, and this is costing you. Tell Vinnie I said hi, and I guess I'll see you soon."

12

Lord of all pots and pans and things
Since I've not time to be
A saint by doing lovely things
Or watching late with Thee
Or dreaming in the dawn light
Or storming heaven's gates
Make me a saint by getting meals
And washing up the plates.

That old Kitchen Prayer beside the stove was framed in crossed pieces of mahogany with a carved leaf at each corner. The illustration depicted a young homemaker standing at the sink, up to her elbows in pretty soapsuds tinged with blue and pink, which always reminded me of the kind of clouds you'd see in a painting of the Assumption. Over her pale green dress, the young homemaker wore a white apron, tied at the waist in a fat bow. Her curly blonde head was turned. She was looking over her shoulder at the drain board, at the dishes gleaming white as the suds, a bubble twinkling on each of them.

The first time I put Mary Kate to work washing the dishes — at the age of about eight — she used so much detergent the suds were piled nearly to her little shoulders in the sink. And she wasn't rinsing, but allowing the bubbles to slide down the plates in gobs to the drain board. When I corrected her, she pouted and pointed to the Kitchen Prayer on the wall, and the lady washing dishes with all those bubbles.

"Well that's not the right way," I had to say — firmly, because that was the only way to handle her when she got that look on her face. "Whoever painted that picture doesn't know anything about washing the dishes. You don't want your supper to taste like soap, do you?"

Years later, when Mary Kate was home from college, she stood in front of the stove and read the Kitchen Prayer out loud for the amusement of her roommate Agnes, who had come home with her for the weekend. Agnes was a broad-faced Irish girl, very pleasant. I had liked her instantly.

Agnes laughed, and said that her grandmother had that same prayer hanging in her kitchen, back home in Staten Island.

Mary Kate rolled her eyes. "The sainted homemaker in her ruffled apron. It's a wonder she's not barefoot and pregnant."

Agnes was a religion major. "You recognize the reference, don't you?" she said. "It's about Martha and Mary. Mary's the one doing the lovely things with Jesus. But poor Martha's the one who gets stuck with the dishes."

I knew the prayer had to do with Martha, the one who came to Jesus complaining that her sister Mary wouldn't help in the kitchen. That story was a actually a favorite of mine, though I never liked the way the priests used Martha in their sermons, as though Jesus were reprimanding her, as though the idea of the story were to demonstrate how Martha had missed the point. In those sermons, it was Mary who was held up as a saint — Mary, who was having a grand old time, hanging onto Jesus' every word while the grease congealed on the dinner plates.

I had my own interpretation, which was that Jesus was human too and liked a good meal as much as the next man. He appreciated Martha's cooking and how she looked out for him. When he said, "Mary has chosen the better part," he wasn't holding up Mary as any model of virtue, but simply acknowledging that she'd gotten the better deal. Mary was probably smart, but not much of a cook. I figured Jesus was fond of both sisters, but maybe, secretly, a little more of Martha.

❍

They couldn't save the tip of the little finger on the Vincent's right hand, and so they amputated it. Only the tip of the finger, I kept telling myself, though I was worried sick.

The day before Barbara was to arrive, Vincent ran a fever. I headed up to the ward early to see how he was doing, and as I passed the open door to the Cube, I looked in and saw Pete sitting in a wheelchair. He was facing away from me, and for one wildly hopeful second he looked exactly the same as he did the first time we spoke to each other, the day he said *You can come over and visit with me*. I half expected him to turn and wave to me.

Then I saw the bandaged stumps propped out in front.

I didn't let it knock me over. I kept moving. *All right, so the feet are gone*, I told myself. *He's up in the chair again, a good sign*. But I knew very well that on the burn ward it was standard practice to get just about everybody up in the chair, critically ill or not, because it was good for the circulation and the lungs, and for a lot of other things I probably wasn't aware of. On the burn ward, a person could approach death just as easily sitting up as lying down.

Vincent burst into tears the minute he saw me. "I can't take it," he cried. "I'm losing my mind."

The ward itself was unusually quiet. All the boys on his side of the room seemed to have been to the tank already, all of them up in the chair, except for Jimmy, who was lying in bed with his comic books. Sergeant Berry was making rounds in the other ward. Someone was playing a radio, the Beatles launching into something perky: *Lady Madonna, children at your feet.*

"What is it?" I asked. "What can't you take?"

"Remember Pete?" he said, and dropped his head and cried.

I'd seen him cry in pain more times that I'd want to count, but there was a convulsive grief in this weeping that was terrible to see. He was so exposed in it. He couldn't hide his face in his hands, couldn't bend his elbows that far.

I put my hand on his head. "It'll be all right," I said. "Pete's strong. He'll be OK."

He glared at me through his tears. "What do you know about it, Mom?" he said. "You're such a goddamned rock. But you know what? — You don't know shit."

It was as though he'd bitten my hand. Tear sprang to my eyes, and I backed away.

Sergeant Berry came over. "Take it easy, soldier," he said. "That's no way to talk to your mother." He winked at me. "We're not having a good day. We just took a walk up the hall. Maybe a little too much too soon."

"I wish you'd just go home," Vincent said, and I was certain he meant Baltimore, not the guesthouse.

Sergeant Berry gave an exaggerated wave goodbye from behind Vincent's back. "Come on, son," he said. "Let's get you back to bed."

I walked without thinking, out of the hospital, past the guesthouse, all the way down the road and through the gate. A city bus pulled up to let someone off, and I stepped aboard, not caring where the bus was headed. I was hurt and tired, and wanted nothing more than to sit by the window. I thought I'd ride to the end of the line, turn around and ride back. Maybe by then the ache in my throat would be gone.

The bus was headed downtown. We crossed the winding, narrow San Antonio River, crossed another part of it, and I remembered the cathedral. I went forward and asked the driver if it were nearby, and he told me to get off right there and walk a couple blocks up and over.

When I arrived at the cathedral, there were almost as many people crossing the plaza and passing through the dark wood arches as there had been on Sunday. I followed an old woman in a black mantilla across the tiles and into the nave. The whole place was humming with big floor fans. Tourists were drifting down the side aisles past the statues and the flickering votive candles. But scattered all over, in the dark worn pews, was a constellation of others who were perfectly still, bent in prayer — old women, a surprising number of men in work clothes, and younger women with children clambering about their skirts.

I drifted with the tourists, past the coffin holding the remains of Crockett and the other defenders of the Alamo, past the statue of San Fernando, the statue of San Antonio. Everywhere there were small bouquets, cut flowers in jars, plastic flowers, single roses lying limp against the feet of the saints. Everywhere there were tokens of petition. Rosaries, obituary clippings, photographs of soldiers and couples and newborn babies, notes written in Spanish and in English — *Nuestra Senora del Perpetuo Socorro . . . Please, God . . . Dear San Antonio de Padua.*

I lit two votive candles, one for Vincent and one for Pete. I knelt down in a pew beside the statue of the Blessed Mother holding the broken body of Jesus. In the flickering light, Jesus' limbs seemed to glisten like sweat. His mother cradled his limp neck with her one hand and held onto his arm with the other. Her face, slightly turned away from the light, was patient and forbearing. Or was it hard as the stone she was carved from?

I remembered the awful day when Vincent was crying in pain. Even on that day I'd held steady. Did that mean I was a *goddamned rock?*

You don't know shit.

But I did know. Maybe I didn't know the complicated politics that had put my youngest child in a helicopter halfway around the earth, but certainly I knew plenty about what happens to that child when the helicopter gets shot down. And I hadn't allowed myself to look away. I'd stood firm, and told him everything would be all right.

The bottom panels of the stained glass windows had been tilted open to let in the air. Beyond them I could hear a rumble of thunder, and then a sudden heavy rush of another afternoon storm. I watched while an old man with a pole made his way from window to window, closing them with a squeak and a thud. I looked back at the statue — the dead son draped across the arms of his mother — and wondered for the first time in my life why an artist would render the scene like that. Hadn't the mother of Jesus been standing off to the side, and then hadn't she more or less disappeared from the story, even from the happy part on Easter morning? Where was it ever mentioned in the gospel that she got to hold her child after he died on the cross?

I took out my rosary, the little white one I'd convinced myself once belonged to Vincent. After I had prayed all the mysteries, I slipped from the pew and went up to the statue. There was a photograph of a newborn baby at the Blessed Mother's feet. Someone had printed the name — *Rosemarie* — above the baby's bald head. The lettering made a perfect little crown. I settled the rosary beside the photograph, and left it there.

Afterwards, I stood in the vestibule, looking out the open door at the rain shower raking hard through the trees and pots of flowers in the square. There was nowhere for me to go. I wasn't ready to go back to the burn ward and Vincent, and at the guesthouse there would be nothing to do but sit and make phone calls home, if I could scrounge up the quarters.

The shower stopped as suddenly as it began, and I took the bus back. When I got to the guesthouse — hours after I'd left Vincent, almost time for dinner — I noticed the yellow Mustang parked at the curb. A day earlier it might have made me happy to know that Caroline had found the strength to come back. But now I was sure her arrival could only mean bad news.

Going into the hospital, I saw Hal.

"Are you all right?" he asked. "I heard it was a rough day."

"I'm all right, but it was hard when he called me a goddamned rock."

It was a shock to hear those words come out of my own mouth, but Hal barely reacted. "Well, you know he didn't mean it," he said. "Sometimes, no matter what you do, it isn't going to suit. You can't win when there's this much pain involved."

He offered to go up to the ward with me, but I said I'd manage on my own.

In the end, I didn't get to see Vincent anyway. He was receiving some sort of treatment, and they sent me away.

As I passed the waiting room, I was surprised to see Ann Bukowsky, standing by the window, dressed not in the usual scrub gown, but in the short-sleeved, green cord summer uniform that the nurses would wear when they weren't working in the hospital. I went over to join her at the window, and she told me she was going on leave for a few days.

"Good for you," I said.

Below, parked in the circle, I saw the white car, the husband standing on the curb, leaning against the door. Four stories below, but I could sense the tension.

She sighed and turned from the window. That's when I noticed the small bruises, four purple fingerprints in a row along the back of the arm, not quite hidden by the short sleeve.

"Are you going home for your leave?" I asked.

"No." As she backed away from the window, I saw a larger bruise — the thumbprint — on the front of the arm. "It's a short leave. If we flew home there would be all that rushing around to see the family and everything."

I did what I usually do when I'm at a loss for the right thing to say — I chattered. I kept my eyes straight over the palm trees circling the parking lot and chattered about how suddenly it had rained, and that was a problem for people with hair like mine, and how I'd heard someone say the weather was going to be pretty for the next few days, and wasn't it nice she'd be off work. "You deserve a little vacation," I said. "You work very hard. But Vincent and I will miss you, of course."

She kept folding and unfolding her hat.

"How long have you been in the Army?" I asked.

"About a year." She explained that she'd actually requested Vietnam, since her husband Phil was over there, but before she could get there he was wounded. They had changed her orders to Fort Sam Houston, because they often did that, so married couples could be together.

"I'm sorry he was hurt," I said. "But it's good you're together."

"He's doing better now," she said, "but he still has a lot of trouble with his leg. It's been such a blow to him. He wanted to stay in the Army, but the medical board put him out." She was moving toward the elevator, settling the hat on her head. "You take care of Vincent now, 'til I get back."

It was like seeing someone caught in a current, someone moving fast out of reach. It was like standing there on the riverbank, helpless.

"Maybe a trip home would be a good thing for you," I said, following her. "Maybe you need to be around other people, family especially, since your husband's having such a hard time of it."

I knew that wasn't quite right. Even in a room full of friends and family, it would still be just the two of them, entirely walled off by their secrets. I knew all about secrets in a marriage.

She pressed the button for the elevator. "Thank you, Mrs. Duvall, but you shouldn't worry. Phil's a good person. Right now he's hurt, that's all."

I glanced quickly at the bruised arm. "If you ever want to talk to me about it. . . ."

"Thank you," she said again.

This is what I was thinking as the elevator doors closed on her: Even good people have a way of flailing about when the hurt is bad enough, and you had better not stand too close. Still, it seemed to me that every young man on the burn ward ought to have someone strong like Ann, someone who wouldn't bail out.

13

No one ever said it back then — at least not to me — but it was a fact that my son Jack was the spitting image of his father. He had Frank's narrow face, his dark coloring and lanky frame. But in temperament he was more like me. For all his lean, dark looks, he was even-tempered, and solidly predictable. As a child, he had not been particularly outgoing, but I never had to worry, for there were always friends calling from the alley for him to come and play, and calling on the phone later, when he was in high school.

At the dinner table, he took on the role of the watchful one. He knew when the boat had been rocked. Like me, he was expert at steering the conversation in safer directions, particularly when Mary Kate would veer into anti-war and anti-draft territories.

One Sunday dinner when Vincent was still at home with us, Mary Kate got up on her high horse.

"So, what do you think about the draft, Jack?" she said. "OK, so you'll get your deferment, and maybe they won't get their hands on you. But you must have an opinion."

"Let's not get off on that," Jack said.

"But that's the problem, don't you see?" She threw a wild, angry look around the table to take us all in. "You never want to talk about it. What about the lottery? Soon as you graduate they could throw you in the hat."

"Jack's applying for medical school," I said. "They can't pull him out of medical school, can they?"

She shot me a furious look and threw her hands up. "Oh my God, Mom, that's exactly what I'm talking about. You think that's OK? — Give Joe College here a break but throw Vinnie to the dogs?"

"That will be enough, Mary Kate," I said.

Vincent just laughed. "Loosen up, people," he said, snatching the last piece of fried chicken from the plate.

Jack left the table and went to the kitchen.

"You're not going to answer me?" Mary Kate called after him.

❍

I got off the elevator in the late afternoon, and was stopped in my tracks. There was Jack, standing in the middle of the waiting room.

"Surprise," he said, stepping forward to give me a kiss, his scruffy sideburns brushing against my cheek. Then he seemed to realize the occasion called for a serious face and dropped the smile. "This is Barbara Houck, Mom. We flew down together."

I hadn't seen the girl, but there she was, getting up from her chair now — a pretty girl with thick blonde hair sweeping her shoulders and framing her face and wide blue eyes. "Didn't this work out great?" she said, with a dimpled smile.

I was surprised speechless.

"I decided at the last minute," Jack said. "I didn't want you to worry. I wanted to see Vinnie, Mom. And this way Barbara and I could fly down together."

"It worked out great," Barbara said again, as though she thought I might need some encouragement.

"Have you been in to see him?" I asked.

"We were waiting for you," Jack said.

I looked from one to the other: Jack, so obviously pleased with himself, and Vincent's little girlfriend Barbara, sweet and scrubbed as a Breck girl off the back of *Good Housekeeping* magazine. It was going to be hard to lead them down that corridor with its oppressive smells and sounds, past the Cube and the chaotic nurses' station.

"Vincent wasn't feeling well this morning," I said. "I'd better check with the nurses."

"Good idea," Barbara said. "And if it's not OK, we can come back in the morning."

I found Colonel Anderson talking to one of the doctors. "Hi, Mrs. Duvall," she said. "I hear Vincent has some visitors."

"But he's been so upset," I said. "Do you think it's a good idea right now?"

"It's a very good idea," she said, and glided out to the waiting room on her silent white shoes to gather up Jack and Barbara as gracefully as she'd gathered me up on the first day. In no time she had them washed and gowned, and we all were heading into the ward. I heard Barbara telling her about nursing school. The colonel asked if the nuns still did the teaching and Barbara answered that the nuns still did the nursing courses, but the other things were taught at the junior college.

Jack walked behind, glancing furtively left and right. The doors to the Cube were closed, but from the ward came the sound of someone calling *Please, nurse, please.*

It was too much to hope that Vincent would be in bed with the burns tucked out of sight. He was sitting up, and when he saw us coming he half-rose to his feet, his splinted arms cranking up and down. He winced, catching his lip, but the smile survived.

"Hey, you made it," he said, looking from Barbara to Jack, and back to Barbara. He didn't seem surprised to see them. "I knew you'd come," he said to Jack. "I told Barb, Call Jack, he'll get you here."

"And here we are," Barbara said, wiping her eyes, leaving identical mascara smudges under her eyes. She leaned over and gave Vincent a kiss on the cheek, daintily holding her hands out. "Oops," she said, stepping back, glancing at Colonel Anderson. "I hope I didn't break any rules in isolation technique."

"Your technique's fine, Dear," the colonel said, and left us.

Isolation — On that crowded little ward, where patients slept and ate and cried entirely without privacy, where visitors had to draw their chairs up close to keep out of the way, the irony was that Vincent's hands could neither touch nor be touched, at least not by those who loved him. I remembered what Dr. Caruso said about Vincent being young and healthy, in his prime. I'd been haunted by memories of his hands when they were healthy — tinkering with his model airplanes, playing that old guitar, and hardest of all, that breathless moment in the gymnasium, when his hands would be suspended in the air, after he made the perfect shot and the ball slipped through the net.

I looked at Barbara, a beautiful girl, laughing softly now, shaking her hair. I was thinking that even when the surgical gowns and gloves became a thing of the past, even when Vincent could reach again and clasp firmly, his hands might never be able to feel as they were meant to. I was thinking that his hands might be stiff forever, incapable of tenderness, or sensing it in the touch of someone who loved him.

"So how's it going, little brother?" Jack asked. He pulled up a chair for Barbara and glanced around for another. "You raising hell down here yet?"

Vincent laughed. "I try."

I borrowed a chair from across the room for Jack, and said I'd be out in the waiting room. They hardly noticed my leaving. Barbara was talking about the flight from Baltimore, Vincent was intent on Barbara, and Jack was leaning forward, elbows on his knees, taking it all in: the ward crammed with equipment, the other patients — just kids, his age or younger — and his brother's hands in the strange splints with the hooks rigged up to tension chords, the little finger on his right hand nothing but a stub now.

When I passed the nurses' station, Colonel Anderson came out from the behind the desk. "Did you know Lieutenant Christie's sweetheart is here again?" she said. "Your young people would be good company for her."

"I'll be sure to introduce them," I said.

As I headed for the waiting room, the corpsmen were just maneuvering a stretcher out of the Cube, and I got a glimpse of the nurses and corpsmen moving around Pete's bed and all those intravenous poles and machines. It struck me then the Cube was the inner chamber in the burn ward — such a small room, but aching with sorrow from wall to wall. I had been in there — the one time, to visit Pete — but I had only a vague memory of how the room was laid out. How many beds, how many windows? I'd been unable to carry the details out with me, and perhaps that was for the best.

The corpsmen were pushing the soldier on the stretcher through the ward now, heading for the tank room, where his wounds would be debrided. The tank room was truly the inner chamber of the burn ward. It was the one room on the burn ward I would never see, for they would never allow a mother to go back there and witness the cruel work of debridement, which I knew would have to be sickening and bloody. All I would ever know of the tank room was the sound of it, the cries that sometimes penetrated the doors.

Caroline was in the waiting room. When I sat down beside her she looked at me with tears in her eyes. "What should I do, Mrs. Duvall?"

Now, now . . . Everything will be all right. The words rose automatically, but I did not say them.

"You're here," I said. "I don't know what else you can do but just be here." I couldn't bring myself to tell her to pray. "What about his family?" I asked. "His mother — Have you called her?"

She shook her head. "I don't really know her."

"Still, maybe you should call," I said. "Just tell her you're here. Pete would like that. You can tell him, when you go back in the Cube. Tell him you talked to his mother."

She straightened up and looked at me hard.

"He can hear you," I said. "No matter how bad it gets, you have to believe he can hear you."

"OK," she said abruptly, and headed for the elevator without even looking back to wave goodbye.

It was nearly dark by the time we got Barbara and Jack signed into the guesthouse and settled in their rooms. They both changed into shorts, and then we went out to the parlor. It was stuffy in the parlor, so I went about cranking open the casement windows and turning on the fans. Cooler air moved in, cooler than it had been in days.

"Feel that air?" Barbara said from the sofa. "Isn't it wonderful?" She leaned back and pulled her bare feet under her. Her hair was brushed off her neck and lopsidedly wrapped with a band. At home they would have been out with friends, to the movies, or to someone's house where there would be a stack of records on the stereo, and maybe some beer and pretzels.

I listened while they talked about Vincent, one making an observation, and the other making the same observation in a slightly different way, as though they needed to see what matched up. I was glad they had come down to see him together.

A little later, I saw Caroline coming in from the hospital, and I called her over to make the introductions. Jack stood up and shook her hand. Barbara patted the sofa and said, "Here, sit down for a while. You must be exhausted."

Caroline's face was pale and puffy. The surgical mask had left a line across her left cheek. She sat down, and almost immediately the three of them were comfortable with each other. I excused myself, saying I was tired, and when I left they were all agreeing they were tired too, that it wouldn't be long before they'd be off to bed.

But the next morning, on the way over to the hospital, I found out otherwise. The story went that some time around midnight the three of them had decided to go out for a ride in Pete's convertible. They had gone off-post for hamburgers at an all-night place, and then, coming back through the gate, had gotten pulled over and questioned by the military police.

"That Caroline's a character," Barbara said. "You should have seen her turn on the charm for those guys."

"Too bad Vinnie missed out," Jack said. "Maybe we shouldn't mention it. It might make him feel bad."

I was walking a little ahead of them, and had to turn to see their faces. Barbara was frowning, thinking it over. "I think we should tell him," she said. "He'll love it."

Up on the ward, she told the story to Vincent with even more drama. Vincent did love it, especially when she widened her eyes and said, "Oh my God, Vinnie, I was scared to death. Military policemen — three of them."

Vincent pretended to be offended. "Hey," he said, scooting forward to nudge her ankle with his bare foot. "Where's my hamburger?"

She turned to me. "Do you think they'd let us do that — bring him a hamburger, or a shake or something?"

Sergeant Berry looked up from straightening the sheets on Jimmy's bed. "If you can get it past the desk," he said, "we'll let him eat it, ma'am."

When they came to take Vincent to the tank, we had to go out to the waiting room. As we passed the Cube, I saw Hal standing in the doorway. He looked me in the eye, and shook his head.

I knew then that Pete had died.

I glanced into the Cube and saw Caroline in there. Colonel Anderson and another nurse had their arms around her. I felt the pain going up from my breast to my throat. I thought of Pete's mother, and wondered how soon the sorrow would arrive at her door.

"I think we've lost Pete," I said quietly to Jack and Barbara, when we got out to the waiting room.

"Why?" Barbara said, looking back in the direction of the closed doors. "What did you see?"

Before I could answer, Caroline came through the doors. I could see she'd had a fast and furious cry, and now she was in the run mode. Jack and Barbara and I stood awkwardly off to the side while Colonel Anderson held Caroline's hand, and Hal urged her sit down. But Caroline only wanted to get out of there.

"Let me walk you to the guesthouse," Hal said.

"I'll go with you," I said, stepping forward.

Caroline just shrugged, and headed for the elevator.

Jack and Barbara held back, one as bewildered as the other. "We'll stay here," Barbara said, her voice wobbling into a question, "and wait for Vinnie?"

"Yes," I said. "That would be best."

When the three of us — Hal and I, with Caroline between us — stepped through the main doors of the hospital, I couldn't help but note what a fine day it was. A front of cool air had blown through during the night, leaving the sky a clean-swept blue, and everything below it sharp in the light. In the distance I could hear parade music, a band marching down the field perhaps, beyond the barracks. *Things'll look better in the morning. You'll see.* Smiling, handsome Pete had died on a jarringly lovely morning in Fort Sam Houston, and the troops marched on, to music.

"I can have someone drive you home," Hal said.

"That's all right, " Caroline said woodenly. "I have Pete's car."

"I see." He nodded earnestly. "We could look after that for you. I don't like to think of you going alone."

"It's not that far. I've driven it many times."

He looked to me.

"He's right, Caroline," I said. "You shouldn't go alone. Not at a time like this. "

She didn't answer, and we walked on in silence. When we were almost to the guesthouse, Jack came bounding across the lawn to catch up with us. "Caroline," he said, out of breath. "Let me ride home with you and keep you company.'

The timing was too perfect. The whole day seemed to have undergone a strange compression.

"It's a good idea," I said quickly. "We'd all feel better if you went along with her. But how would you get back here, Jack?"

"That's not a problem," Hal said. "I'll send someone up to get him."

There was Pete's yellow Mustang parked in front of the guesthouse, and there was the road glimmering in the sunshine. I'd hardly taken in Jack's sudden appearance in San Antonio, and now he was about to ride off through the hills for Austin. And Pete was dead. The day kept speeding crazily, and the next thing I knew, Jack was setting Caroline's bag in the back seat of the Mustang, and she was hugging me goodbye, knocking those big sunglasses sideways on her face.

"I'll see you tonight, Mom," Jack said, getting behind the wheel.

"Call me when you get there," Hal said, handing Jack a card. "Here's the number."

"I'll be thinking of you, Caroline," I said.

Caroline smiled at me wanly. "Just so you know, Mrs. Duvall — I talked to him, like you said."

"That's good, honey," I said. "He heard you."

Hal and I watched the Mustang move slowly down the post road and out of view, and then we went back to the ward. When we got off the elevator on the fourth floor Barbara was there, standing at the window of the waiting room. She had probably watched our approach across the lawn. "They're doing some sort of dressing on Vinnie," she said, "and I had to wait out here. But he knows about Pete."

"It's good you were with him," Hal said.

"How is he?" I asked.

"OK," she said, blinking back the tears. "I think he's OK."

Just then Corporal Jenks poked his head out the doors, and called "OK" in our direction, like a strange little echo, and back we went to Vincent. He was already working on his lunch tray. He raised his fork contraption in a salute, his eyes fixed on Barbara.

Jack was back from Austin before sundown. He drove himself in a red Chevrolet with fins, which he said belonged to Caroline. This confused me, and I asked how we would now get that car back to Caroline.

"Don't worry about it, Mom," he said.

"So how did it go?" I asked. "Was she all right?"

"She's OK," he said. "Her mother came over."

14

I wrote a letter to Pete's mother. I used the stationery I bought in the gift shop, good cream-colored paper with a small pen and ink drawing of the Alamo centered at the top. Plain paper would have been more appropriate for a condolence note, but I told myself that if I were in Mrs. Christie's place, I wouldn't be thinking about something like that.

I wrote that everyone had loved Pete, that he had been kind to Vincent, to all the young men on the ward. "He was particularly kind to me," I wrote.

If Vincent had died, and if I hadn't gotten to him in time, I'd have been desperate to find more than that written under the drawing of the Alamo, under the terrible date. I'd have wanted to know that he didn't suffer, that he didn't cry my name when he was out of his head with pain. But I'd seen with my own eyes how Pete really had suffered. And who could know what he cried in his heart?

"I will never forget your son Pete," I wrote in the end, above my name.

I gave the letter to Colonel Anderson.

"How kind of you," she said, and put the letter in her starched pocket. "I'll see that it gets to her."

❍

Life goes on: meaning, to my way of thinking, you ought to take comfort in what you haven't lost. But on the burn ward, something more was always being lost — eschar cut away, parts of fingers, hands and feet, whole limbs. And precious lives.

During the short time that Jack and Barbara were visiting, five new patients arrived on a flight from Japan, three of them very severely burned. We would hurry past the open doors of the Cube, trying not to look in. The nurses and corpsmen flew back and forth, working long and extra shifts, joking grimly with each other from behind their masks. *Life goes on, precariously.* The workers had no time to weep over the ones they'd lost.

Every time I passed the Cube, I'd think of Pete, the sadness rolling over me, a physical sensation, a genuine ache.

The nurses and doctors had others to run for now, others to suction and turn and slather with Sulfamylon, to lower into the tank and cart back onto the wards again. Hal and Father Smith were busy too, moving as always from bed to bed in the Cube.

The first to die was the one most severely burned, over seventy per cent of his body. I heard that he was only seventeen years old, which meant that his parents must have signed the papers for him to enlist. Then they lost the one in the bed closest to the door, the one who had seemed to me the least severely burned. Once, when I glanced in, this boy had surprised me by lifting his hand to wave. But he died the second night, from a sudden respiratory complication, or so I heard.

Meanwhile Jack and Barbara turned on the little transistor radio they'd brought along, and they even played cards, though only a couple of hands at a time, because Vincent tired easily. Barbara shuffled and dealt with an exaggerated flair, her pink-painted nails flashing delicately. She arranged Vincent's cards, holding them up for him, swearing that she wasn't looking. Vincent rolled his eyes and said, "Yeah, sure you aren't."

Jack would talk to the other patients. He pushed Jimmy around in the wheelchair. Once he had a nice chat with Dr. Nuttell about his applications for medical school. Meanwhile, Ann Bukowsky returned from her leave, looking thinner than ever, and Dr. Caruso returned from Japan to assume his usual place in the flock on rounds.

I tried to keep to the background, and let Barbara take over the meal tray. She'd put the surgical gown on, fussing the whole time that Vincent wouldn't even get to see what she was wearing. Then she'd set to work with the seriousness of a little general, spooning all the sherbet from the edges of the cup, shaking the juice cartons to make sure Vincent had sucked up every last drop.

"That would be five hundred sixty cc's," she said, when Sergeant Berry came around with fluid chart. "A carton of milk, a small glass of grape juice, and this much water."

"She's a nurse," Vincent said.

"A student nurse," she said.

"Is that right?" Sergeant Berry said. "You going to sign up when you graduate? They'll make you a second lieutenant right off the bat, you know."

"I don't think so," she said, rolling her eyes at Vincent.

But later, when we were walking back to the guesthouse, she said she found it interesting that Colonel Anderson outranked most of the doctors. She laughed and said that the nuns at the nursing school had taught them to stand up the moment a doctor entered the room. "So in the Army I guess it can be the other way around," she said. "Vincent's doctor must have to stand up for Colonel Anderson." This seemed to tickle her pink.

"I wouldn't know," I said, "because Dr. Caruso hardly ever sits down."

"Actually I think he has to salute her," she said with frown.

I noticed that Lieutenant Darby never once cautioned Barbara about doing too much for Vincent, not even when he saw her leaning over Vincent, holding the straw for him. "Way to go, Vince," he said, smiling at Barbara. "Drink those fluids."

Too soon it was time for Barbara and Jack to fly home. On the afternoon of their last day, I suggested that Jack and I take a little walk. It was hot, and so we walked slowly, talking about the classes he'd be taking in the fall. He was worried about Biochemistry and said he didn't even know if it was worth applying for medical school. Apparently his advisor at Loyola hadn't been encouraging.

"You'll get in," I said. "You just need to ask your grandmother to put you on the prayer list."

He laughed. "Yeah — the St. Jude list. It's a hopeless case."

"No it's not," I said. "But they can't draft you in the mean time, can they?"

He shrugged. "They say they'll have a lottery before the end of the year. Don't get yourself worried about it, Mom. There's nothing we can do anyway."

We went off post, the route I usually followed. When we arrived at my favorite park, we saw a small crowd had gathered there. Several rows of folding chairs had been arranged to face a stage area of sorts, under a canopy. The atmosphere was serious — no kids running around, no ice cream truck. In the shade of the trees, there was a card table set up, where a girl in a bandana and long gauze skirt was methodically filling paper cups from a big pitcher. "Lemonade?" she called to us. "It's free."

Jack declined, but I took a cup. The lemonade was tepid, the powdered kind, and rather weak.

"What's the occasion?" Jack asked.

"We've got three distinguished speakers lined up," the girl said proudly. "Anti-war, of course."

A San Antonio police car eased around the corner. The girl took note. "Ben!" she called over her shoulder, and the man fiddling with the microphone under the canopy looked up.

Meanwhile, an older woman in a professional-looking pants suit stepped up to the table and flung her leather bag wearily on the grass. "God, it's hot," she said. "Do you know who's organizing this shindig? I'm from *The Light*."

The girl pointed in the direction of the microphones. "Over there. Ask for Ben."

"Is Father O'Malley speaking?"

"He is." The girl smiled. "Any minute now."

The reporter didn't smile back. She swung her bag onto her shoulder, picked up a cup of lemonade, and headed for Ben.

"Who's Father O'Malley?" Jack asked.

"He's a Jesuit, a peace activist," the girl answered, still watching the progress of the reporter. "He's out on bail for anti-draft stuff in Washington."

"That should make for an interesting article."

"You bet." The girl winked, and went back to pouring lemonade.

We took up circling again. We passed the policemen, on the other side now, standing against their car in the shade.

"Hot afternoon for a rally," one of them said pleasantly.

"Yes," I said. It was very hot, and I wanted to head back.

But Jack turned in the direction of the stage, and so I followed.

In the crowd under the canopy there was no sign of a person in a priest's collar. Three people were now seated behind the microphone — two severe-looking young women in plain skirts and blouses, and a balding middle-aged man in a T-shirt and slacks. The man named Ben stepped up the microphone, gave it a couple of thumps, and suggested that the folks standing around on the grass have a seat. A handful responded. There were about forty people in the audience.

"And now, with no further ado, allow me to introduce our first speaker, Father James O'Malley."

The man in the T-shirt stood up, shook Ben's hand, and waved to the crowd. The people in the chairs stood up and applauded. The two women behind him applauded too, their frowns more severe than ever.

"Thank you. Thank you, my dear friends," Father O'Malley said, closing his eyes and gripping the podium. For a moment I thought he was about to begin with a prayer. But apparently he hadn't come to pray. "Let me begin," he said, his eyes sweeping slowly over the audience, "with the reason we chose this beautiful city of yours as our first stop. San Antonio, my dear friends, happens to be a city of five military bases, a city representative of the strong and alarming wave of militarism overtaking our whole country." His accent reminded me of John F. Kennedy. After every other sentence, there would be a clatter of applause.

This war . . . this war . . . illegal . . . immoral . . . this war . . . inconsistent with the true American values. The very words Mary Kate would fling across the dinner table at home. Here was a priest after Mary Kate's own heart.

The girl from the lemonade stand approached us, clapping with the rest of the crowd, her bracelets jingling down her arm.

"Plenty of seats," she said to Jack. "Don't you want to sit down?"

"No thanks," he said. "We can't stay. My brother's in the hospital on post."

"I'm sorry. I hope he's O.K."

"He's not."

She averted her eyes, looking adolescent and uncomfortable. "I'm really sorry," she said, and went back to her lemonade.

After a while, the priest turned the microphone over to one of the women. I saw that she wasn't as old as I'd thought. She was probably closer in age to Jack. She took no time to smile at the crowd. "I'll tell you what the draft is," she said, her face so close to the microphone her words sizzled. "It's slavery. Slavery — in the land of the free."

"Let's go," I said, for I'd had enough.

But Jack was rooted.

"Nobody gives a damn," the girl spat into the microphone. "Do you think the white college kids in this town give a shit if some Mexican boy gets drafted? The white kids are busy with their frat parties. So what if a kid from across town gets blown to pieces in Vietnam?"

Jack breathed in hard, like he'd been punched, then took off at such a stride I had to run to keep up. When he got as far as the corner, he stopped, not to wait for me but to stare back at the canopy. The loudspeaker was still spewing out the young woman's anger. Jack's face was screwed up with the effort not to cry.

I took him by the arm.

"Jesus Christ," he cried, pulling away from me. "How can you stand it, Mom?"

"How can I stand what?"

He stared back at me. "How can you stand to look at Vinnie?" His voice was so choked it came out in a whisper.

"You have to look at him too, Jack," I said gently. "How do you stand it?"

He walked away, and I followed. I kept talking, the way I would at home whenever there was some unpleasantness at the dinner table and we all just needed to get past it. I talked mindlessly about the heat, and whether or not they would serve grits in the mess hall again for dinner. I was desperate not to hurt him. Something about the levelness in my own voice felt wrong, and yet I didn't know what else to do to comfort the child after my own heart, the steady one who preferred not to rock the boat.

We went through the post gate, and came to a bench. I sat down, and Jack sat beside me without a word.

"Listen," I said. "Vincent was drafted, and you weren't. That doesn't make it your fault."

He glanced over his shoulder, as though the park were still in view. "Mary Kate was right, Mom. We should have done something. But we just stood around like dumb sheep and let him go." He dropped his face into his hands. "He's just a kid. He's my little brother."

"But what could we have done?"

He didn't answer.

"What, Jack? What do you think we should have done?"

He lifted his face. "Canada."

"Canada?" He might as well have said Mars.

"You know what I mean, Mom."

It wasn't as though I hadn't read the papers, and didn't know that Canada was where some of the boys would go. "But Sweetheart," I said, and stroked the back of his bowed head, "it wouldn't have occurred to us. We just aren't like that."

He wiped his eyes on the back of his hand. "Well, it occurred to Mary Kate. She had these friends who wanted to help. But of course Vinnie wouldn't have any part of it." He shook his head and gave a short, bitter laugh. "Dumb, stubborn kid."

I'd never seen Canada, but in my mind it was always woodsy and calm. I pictured Vincent sitting by the fire in a remote log cabin, playing his guitar for Mary Kate's friends. It seemed to me an impossible fairy tale in which the precious child gets hidden away in the woods. And what would have been the point anyway, if Vincent would have to stay hidden like that forever, far away in another country — if he could never come home again?

We just aren't like that. Maybe the people who couldn't imagine themselves in the fairy tale were the ones who ended up living the nightmare instead. *Think, Mom.* Or maybe it was the people who didn't think. And if Jack didn't get into medical school, would he end up running away to Canada, never to come home again?

"I didn't know about any of this," I said.

"Of course you didn't. And we wouldn't have told you. At least not until it was done." He stood up and reached out a hand to me. "Let's go. We've been gone a long time."

And so we headed down the main post road toward Brooke Army Medical Center, which was so familiar to me now, shimmering on the horizon at the end of the sunburned field like a fort in some old western movie. We passed yet another platoon of recruits, marching in formation on the other side of the road, and their chanting got mixed up in my head, along with the words from the rally: *blown* to *piec*-es, *blown* to *piec*-es, *no* one *gives* a *damn.*

Up on the ward, Barbara and a corpsman were taking Vincent for a walk. The corpsman — a black man named Parks, who had strong and shining arms — was pushing the I.V. pole. Vincent shuffled between them, his slippers scratching *one-two, one-two* against the linoleum.

"Stand up straight, " Parks said. "Pick up your feet."

"Slave driver," Vincent muttered.

"Who you calling slave driver?" Parks said.

Barbara laughed. She had a surprisingly loud laugh. She had a way of turning heads.

Someone switched on a radio, the volume higher than Sergeant Berry usually allowed. They were playing a catchy country tune with a thumping base and whining fiddles. Barbara put her hand on her hip and sashayed along. Parks slapped his thigh, and did a hopping step.

"Vinnie can play the guitar," Barbara said.

"Is that right?" Parks said.

"He's good too." There wasn't the slightest inflection of regret in her voice.

Vincent was walking along with his shoulders square, a real smile on his face.

Barbara was a smart girl, a student nurse, and she had taken a good hard look at Vincent's hands. And yet she spoke as though she really believed he'd play that guitar again. I hoped with all my heart that my son wouldn't lose this girl, that there wouldn't be some other boy back in Baltimore to steal her away from us, a boy who hadn't been drafted, hadn't been wounded.

Jack and I went to wait outside, and that was when — at the very last minute, of course — he told me he was thinking of taking a semester off.

"I could help with Vinnie when he gets home," he said. "It's not too late to withdraw."

"No," I said firmly, and argued hard and fast that no one expected that from him, that he'd be plenty of help when he wasn't in class, that he just had to go ahead with his applications for medical school, no matter what.

"Right," he said sarcastically. "So I can be the big doctor and do great things for humanity." He shook his head. "So I can avoid the draft too, of course."

"I don't want to hear any more about this," I said. "And remember — Vincent is doing well. You have to concentrate on that. You are proud of your brother, aren't you?"

"Of course I am," he said.

"So you keep telling him that," I said. "And you go on doing what you were doing before."

He picked up a magazine from the table and leafed through it idly. "So Mom — " he said, "do you think we should join Mary Kate and her friends, and burn the American flag on the White House lawn?"

"That's not funny, Jack," I said. "What are you saying? Has she gotten into some kind of trouble?"

"They haven't locked her up yet, if that's what you mean." He gave me a wry smile. "She's coming down here, you know."

This was news to me, though it shouldn't have been. "When?"

"Soon. She said not to worry you with the details."

"How are you affording these plane tickets, Jack?" I asked.

"I'm not supposed to say. But that's kind of stupid, isn't it?" He shook his head. "Dad gave us the money."

"I don't believe it."

"Believe it. He practically insisted."

The doors to the ward opened again — Barbara now, coming toward us.

"I took that stupid gown off in the doorway," she said, her face flushed. "I wanted him to see my dress."

Jack glanced down at the tanned legs below the short skirt. "I bet he wasn't the only one who appreciated that," he said.

She laughed, and shook her hair from her shoulders. "I'm going to send him a picture of me, as soon as I get back."

Late in the evening that day, about the time I was preparing for bed, Jack came to tell me that Caroline had arrived at the guesthouse. A girlfriend of hers had driven her down from Austin to pick up her car. Apparently it had all been arranged in advance, but he had somehow neglected to tell me about it.

When I went out to say hello, my heart sank to see Caroline standing at the curb in her shorts and white sleeveless blouse, her shoulders bare, her dark hair swept up, as it had been in the photograph Pete used to keep beside his bed. Caroline smiled and waved, but she didn't come across the lawn to speak to me. Her girlfriend was sitting behind the wheel of the car, the motor still running.

"I'm just going to ride around with them for a little while," Jack said. "I won't be long."

He strode across the lawn and climbed into the car. As they pulled away, Caroline waved again from the window, and faintly called "Byebye."

15

Sometimes I pictured the part I would play in the happy ending: going home to fill the freezer with casseroles — all of Vincent's favorites — throwing myself into a major cleaning, washing all the curtains, certainly the ones in his bedroom. And then, when the house was spotless and the curtains crisp at the shining windows, at last Vincent would come striding up the front walk with his girlfriend Barbara at his side. And then I'd get carried away and picture the neighbors up and down Constance Avenue out on their porches, waving and cheering.

What would they be cheering for? They wouldn't be cheering that Vincent had served valiantly in Vietnam.

Bring them home! The cry of the protestors seemed so pitiful to me, for what made them think that the harm of sending those boys in the first place could ever be undone? I knew how it would go: We would bring Vincent home to our house on the second block of Constance Avenue, to the entire congregation of St. Anthony's Church — young Vincent Duvall, whose hands had been burned in a war that kept going on somehow, though no one could understand it anymore, if they had understood it in the first place. Vincent Duvall, who had been *burned*. They would all avert their eyes.

❍

After Jack and Barbara went back to Baltimore, Vincent's mood plunged. He took it out on me mostly, in peevishness and short answers. I understood that he was uncomfortable with me hanging on, and yet I wanted to stay, at least until the first skin graft.

One gloomy morning, a Red Cross volunteer arrived with a cart of mail and packages.

"Package for you, Darlin'," she said to Vincent. "You want some help opening it?"

"Sure," Vincent said. "Thanks."

She took a small package from the bottom of her cart, and a pair of scissors from her apron pocket — scissors shaped like a stork, the exact same scissors I had at home in the top drawer of my sewing machine table. She removed the brown paper, and there was the framed photograph of Barbara with her beautiful hair pinned up and a pointed nurse's cap set on top.

"Wow," Vincent said.

"Bless her little heart," the volunteer said. "Here, let's put that right on your table, where you can see it."

That afternoon, Hal asked if I wanted to take a ride off post, an informal field trip to see Mission San Jose with some of the other parents. It was a good idea. I needed time away from Vincent, and more than that, he needed time away from me.

I waited in front of the hospital, with another mother, Rachel Solomon, whose son was downstairs on 13B — a naval officer who'd been burned in a kitchen fire on board ship. Hal arrived in plaid shorts and a yellow shirt. There were already three people in his car. Sitting next to him was a petite Hispanic woman I'd seen once or twice in the Cube, and in the back were Georgia and Buzz Larson, the parents of Jimmy, the boy who was always reading the comics.

Rachel squeezed in with the Larsons, so I got in next to the Hispanic woman. Hal introduced her as Estella, and said she'd come up from Laredo. Estella smiled shyly, and I wondered if she could speak English.

As we headed off post, the Larsons were saying that in the morning they'd be flying back to Indiana, and Jimmy would be coming home by the end of the following week. He would be fitted for his leg prosthesis at the V.A.

"I figure to have him back on the tractor by next spring," Buzz said, winking at me.

"Oh no you won't," Georgia said, like the straight man in the comedy team. "He's getting his diploma, and he's going on to the junior college, if that's the last thing I see to in *my* life."

Apparently it had been a big deal for Buzz to leave the farm at such a crucial time. He said he couldn't have done it if his brother and his two nephews, who lived on a neighboring farm, hadn't stepped up and offered to take over for him.

Now they would go back to the farmhouse in Indiana and take up where they'd left off. I imagined Georgia standing at the stove, the table set with a checkered cloth and a vase of zinnias from the yard, and Buzz coming in from the barn, stomping his boots on the back porch. Jimmy in his wheelchair — no, Jimmy coming back from the barn too, managing his new prosthesis just fine — and Georgia watching his progress from the kitchen window, her heart aching. *Home*.

We were a few miles off post, passing through a neighborhood of small one-story houses. I looked out and saw children playing in a yard, a woman sweeping the steps. There were sheets and a row of diapers hanging on the line along the side. I was thinking of my own home, so far away, the café curtains at the kitchen window, the African violets I hoped Jack would remember to water on the sill.

Hal was speaking carefully to Estella in Spanish. She kept nodding, occasionally answering.

"Not bad, huh?" Hal said. "I've been doing pretty good with my Spanish lately."

Then Rachel leaned forward from the back, and she and Estella spoke excitedly in rapid Spanish.

"Estella's daughter is getting married in December," Rachel said to the rest of us. "She wants to check out Joske's department store while she's here. Maybe find a dress on sale."

Hal laughed. "That's the last time I show off when you're around, Rachel."

It wasn't a long drive before we arrived at Mission San Jose. From the outside it didn't look like much. We got out of the car and followed Hal across the lawn — first the Larsons, then Estella and I, with Rachel bringing up the rear, wheezing and complaining of the heat.

We walked along the old stone and mortar walls of what Hal called the *convento*, and through a garden enclosed in trimmed hedges. He gave us a little of the history, the story of the five Spanish Catholic missions strung along the San Antonio River: Espada, San Juan, San Jose, Concepcion, and San Antonio de Valero — better known as the Alamo. But after that he didn't have much to say, and seemed inclined to stand to the side and let each of us pass ahead of him.

One by one we entered the old rooms, each with a view framed by a deep-set window or doorway: a gnarled live oak, a pot of herbs, a wedge of sky. There were tourists coming and going, but their voices — even the voices of the children — were hushed above the sound of their footsteps on the gravel paths. It was disorienting, like being lifted up from the awful burn ward and dropped into a peaceful dream. I looked out through an arched passageway, which framed even more arches beyond, and I was glad that I'd come.

The Larsons and Estella strolled off in the direction of the garden. Rachel sat down on a low crumbling wall, unfolded a piece of paper from her pocketbook, and proceeded to fan herself furiously.

"Are you OK, Rachel?" Hal asked.

"Hot flash, Love," she said. "Don't pay me any mind."

He turned to me. "Want to climb the stairs?"

I followed him up the sloping stairs of worn stone, and we came to a narrow landing with a window. The view was of a yard shaded by a solitary tree, and a few tourists moving through.

"Thank you for bringing us here, Hal," I said. "It's lovely."

"You're welcome."

In that narrow space our shoulders were nearly touching, and if either of us leaned forward on the window ledge we'd be standing closer still.

"It's so peaceful," I said. "I'd be happy to sit down in any corner of this place, and do nothing at all."

"You ought to go ahead and choose a corner."

I kept my eyes on the yard, on a man walking with his little boy. "Do you have family?" I asked.

"A military family, as a matter of fact," he answered. "My father's a retired colonel, my brother's a lieutenant colonel in the medical service corps, and my sister's married to a West Point graduate." He turned so that he was leaning against the wall, facing me. "And my mother was president of the Officers' Wives' Club so many times they gave her a little bronze gavel with her name on it."

I laughed.

He just smiled, something on his mind. "But I guess you meant am I married," he said.

"Yes."

"I was — once. But by the time I got back from Korea, she'd found someone else."

"I'm sorry," I said.

"We were too young," he said. "Thank God there weren't any children. It put me into a tailspin though, and I got out of the Army. My father about disowned me for that."

"But then you changed your mind, and went back in?"

"Not right away. There were some years in between. First the seminary, and then some years as an assistant pastor in Philadelphia." He glanced away, ill at ease. It was the first time I'd seen him like that, and I was sorry for it.

"So then you came here?" I asked.

"I did a tour in Vietnam first, and then here. From the frying pan into the fire you might say." He smiled at me grimly. "Sorry."

"I didn't know you'd been to Vietnam."

He shrugged. "I survived. At the time it seemed like a good career move."

"But I think it's true what you say," I added quickly. "It is the frying pan into the fire. Just because you're out of danger doesn't necessarily mean it's any easier. Everywhere you look it's something terrible happening. And it just goes on like that, day after day."

He nodded. "One med-evac after another."

"I remember you saying the busy people are the lucky ones," I said. "I have nothing to do up there but look at what's happened to Vincent. When he got sent to Vietnam it was like a catastrophe out of the blue, and all I could do was hold on and wait for it to be over. But now I think — Was it really out of the blue? I have this sense that I wasn't paying attention."

He gave me a crooked smile and shook his head.

"I didn't mean to take over," I said. "We were talking about you."

"I like hearing what's on your mind," he said, "and here's my advice, for what it's worth. Don't be beating yourself up about what you did or didn't do. It's a bad habit. It'll stunt your growth."

"I think it's called examining your conscience," I said grimly. "It's supposed to be good for your soul."

He threw back his head and laughed. "You're funny, Kitty Duvall," he said. "Too bad we don't have time to talk like this more often."

Standing there, shoulder-to-shoulder, we both looked down at the yard, where the Larsons were strolling through, hand in hand.

"There's something I've been meaning to ask," he said. "You've never mentioned your husband. Vincent tells me he lives in Florida."

"He left us years ago," I said evenly.

"You never divorced?"

"I'm a Catholic. What would be the point?"

He nodded thoughtfully. "True. 'Divorced Catholic' does sort of cancel itself out. How can you be both Catholic and divorced, when the Church doesn't really recognize divorce?"

His expression was pleasant as ever, but something had stung me. "I never looked at it that way," I said, "but I guess you're right. It does cancel itself out."

"I'm sorry. I didn't mean to offend."

"No offense."

"So you've been alone — for how many years?"

I had to think. "I guess about twelve years, give or take." I didn't know if I should count the years Frank had gone and then come back.

"A long time," he said.

I backed away. "I want to visit that little chapel down there before we go," I said.

"Good," he said. "You should do that."

And I left him standing there at the window.

In the chapel, I contemplated the altar and the old crucifix with its worn gold figure of Jesus — his arms spread, the little cloth curled decoratively over his privates. I was thinking of the time I heard Vincent scream from the tank room, and what Hal said when we were sitting on the bench outside, about how hard it had been for him the first day on the burn ward, seeing the boy who was burned all over his body, naked and crying in the tank room.

And yet Hal had gone on with what he had to do, praying with the boys, joking around with them, even with the ones who were so sick they couldn't open their eyes and look back at him. His work was nothing like the doctors' and nurses'. He had no beds to strip or dressings to change or surgeries to perform. Day after day, he had to speak words of comfort, standing in for a loving God, which had to be hardest job of all in a sorrowful place like a burn ward.

16

Mary Kate had been ranting about Vietnam since her days at Catholic University, right there in the Capitol, where apparently she could hop into a demonstration on just about any day of the week. At home, in two seconds flat, she could take front and center on the subject of the war, ignoring everything her grandmother and I taught her about polite conversation, nervous red blotches popping up on her face and down her neck. So of course we avoided anything remotely to do with politics when she was around. We avoided to no avail.

Mary Kate joined an anti-war prayer group. One evening, when I stopped by her apartment with a jar of homemade crab soup, I met two members of the group — a priest and a nun. Mary Kate introduced them to me as Father Steve and Sister Cathy. They were both dressed in casual street clothes, but their manner wasn't casual at all. They were very intense young people who talked about politics and the war the whole time I was there, apparently just assuming I'd agree with whatever they had to say.

Mary Kate seemed particularly enthralled with Father Steve. I knew a woman in our parish whose daughter had actually married a priest. And so when I saw Mary Kate gazing into the fiery eyes of Father Steve, all I could think was how hard it would be to live with that — your own daughter the reason a priest had abandoned his vows.

I'd also been reading in the papers about a group of religious people who were continually demonstrating at draft boards and military places like Ft. Holabird in Baltimore. These were the people who had stolen draft records from the Customs House and doused them with blood. They were mostly priests and nuns — Josephite, Jesuit, Maryknoll. There were two women in the group, a nun and a nurse named Moylan, such an Irish-Catholic name, and then there were the famous brothers, Daniel and Philip Berrigan. And all of them determined to get themselves thrown in jail. I couldn't help but worry about what Mary Kate was up to, what she wasn't telling me.

And then in May, when we knew Vincent would be sent to Vietnam for sure, my heart squeezed in my chest to read in the papers how those people — they were calling them the Catonsville Nine then — had set fire to draft records, and how they were all carted away in a paddy wagon. It rattled me to think something like that had happened so close, right down the road in Catonsville, at the end of the old number 8 streetcar line.

In those days it was best not to know what Mary Kate was up to, because there was no one — certainly not me anyway — who could talk any sense into her head. She was clearly distraught about the fate of those nine who were arrested. In October, while the trial was going on, she was down there in the street in front of the Baltimore Post Office, protesting. I knew this because Bonnie told me she'd seen her on the news.

"She was right in front," Bonnie told me. "She was holding a sign that said 'Free the Nine.' It was only a flash, but I'm sure it was Mary Kate. She was wearing that orange scarf we gave her for her birthday."

It all came to a head on Easter, when Vincent had been in Vietnam for four months already. As we were leaving St. Anthony's after Mass, Mary Kate turned on me. "I don't know how you stand coming to this church," she snapped. "When are these priests going to open their mouths and talk about peace?"

We were trapped in the vestibule, the parishioners moving out slowly, because old Father Reilly was holding things up, shaking hands at the door. Everyone was dressed in Easter finery, all those pastel colors, so many women with corsages, my mother wearing the gardenia I ordered for her from Gardenville Florists. Mary Kate had on a ratty black jacket over a navy blue skirt that looked like she might have slept in it. It was not a particularly warm Easter, but her feet — in scuffed brown sandals — were bare.

"They talk about peace all the time," I said carefully. To my relief, Jack had just taken my mother by the elbow, and they were both out of earshot.

"Well, I don't think you can talk about peace and ignore this war," Mary Kate said. "Every priest in the country ought to be out there in the streets, leading the people."

My eyes were on the rack of pamphlets next to the door — *The Sacred Heart Yesterday and Today*, *A Catholic Girl's Guide*, *The Rosary: An Urgent Appeal for Peace*.

"Think, Mom," she said, even louder now, as we stepped out into the light of a beautiful Easter morning, and I saw the forsythia, so intensely yellow, lining the sidewalk across the street. "Your own son is over there now. It isn't enough to sit in the pew and hang onto the rosary beads."

Father Reilly was still shaking hands, outside now at the top of the stairs. He glanced mildly in our direction.

I turned on my heel, and didn't look back until I caught up with Jack and my mother. On the far side of the parking lot I saw Mary Kate's green Volkswagen already tearing away. Typical — Mary Kate getting in the parting shot with those peace symbols plastered all over the bumper and up to the back window.

That year it was my turn to have the Easter dinner. I was expecting my mother and my Aunt Claudette, my sister Bonnie and my brother-in-law Richard and my two little nephews, Tim and Stephen. And Jack and Mary Kate, of course.

Jack was a help getting things on the table and carving the ham, but Mary Kate didn't breeze in until we'd just about cleaned our plates. As she was settling in at the table, I heard her say something in reply to Richard, something about Vincent and the "unjust war."

"Mary Kate," Jack murmured, and cast a warning glance.

"I don't care," she said boldly. "Somebody has to say something."

Richard had served in the Pacific and was an officer in the VFW. He stared at her, his face taking on that high-blood-pressure flush. "Just a minute, young lady," he said. "Let's not forget that your brother is serving his country honorably."

She tossed her napkin on the plate, pushed her chair back, and stomped to the living room, where she grabbed her big canvas bag from the sofa. I thought she was about to leave, but then she was back, holding out something in her hand — a bronze medal, about the size of a silver dollar, with a striped ribbon attached — red, yellow, and green. "Here, Uncle Richard," she cried. "How about this for honorable."

"That's a Vietnam medal," Richard said, taking it from her, studying it. "Where did you get this?"

"On the mall in Washington. There were lots of vets there. They were giving their stuff away."

"Are you telling me that somebody just gave this to you?" he asked, narrowing his eyes at her.

Bonnie put a hand on Richard's forearm, but he pulled away from her, and stood up.

"Yes," Mary Kate said, tilting her chin boldly at him, the uncle who happened to be her godfather, who'd been so proud to hold her the day she was baptized. "He said it made him sick to look at it," she said. "He asked me to throw it away."

Richard took out his handkerchief, wrapped the medal in it, and put it into his breast pocket. He was so angry his hands were shaking.

Tears were running down Mary Kate's face.

"Mary Kate's crying," little Stephen whispered.

"We've got to go home," Richard said, turning to Bonnie. "I can't take much more of this."

But by then Mary Kate was heading for the front door herself, and no one was getting up to go after her.

"Please, Richard," I said. "We can't have Easter end this way."

"You haven't had any coconut cake," my mother said. "I made it just for you, Richard, because it's your favorite."

Bonnie laughed, too loud. "Who do you think you're fooling, Mother?" she said. "Coconut cake isn't Richard's favorite. It's yours."

Richard only shook his head.

"Just let it go," Bonnie said softly to him. "These are hard times."

When he sat down, I looked over at him gratefully, but my heart was aching. Coconut cake was Mary Kate's favorite too, and nobody had run after her, or pleaded with her to come back.

"What does she want from us, Kitty?" Bonnie asked later, when we were carrying the plates to the kitchen. "Nobody likes this war. Nobody even understands it. And we're all just sick about Vincent being over there. Of course Richard gets mad when he sees these young people in ripped-up uniforms, but he's worried about Vinnie being over there too."

"I don't know what she wants," I said, but that was only to close the subject, so we could get on with putting out the desserts, so the whole day would be over with.

After everyone had gone home and I was putting the good dishes away, I stopped to look at the old portrait on the sideboard — me holding baby Mary Kate, a tinted sepia I'd had taken in Hutzler's Department Store downtown. I was twenty-two years old at the time, but in that photograph I look a good deal older. I'm wearing the broad-shouldered suit I was married in. My lips are painted dark, and my hair is anchored in a sophisticated do. Mary Kate, fat and rosy-cheeked, is wearing the pink dress that her Great-aunt Claudette smocked by hand. She isn't exactly smiling. She's staring right at the camera, her little eyebrows dipping slightly — only six months old, and already serious.

O

Dr. Caruso was preparing Vincent for the autografts. I understood it was a step forward, but at the same time it was a step back: New trauma — planned trauma — and with it more pain. They would take Vincent to the operating room and shave strips of healthy skin from the legs with a special instrument called a dermatome. Dr. Caruso would then cut little slices into those healthy strips, making a checkerboard that could be stretched to cover a greater area — making the most of them, in other words. Therefore, in a cruel irony of the burn ward, there would then be two new wounds on the legs, just as raw as the burns themselves. But these new wounds — the donor sites, they were called — would be covered with pieces of mesh fabric, which would be kept damp with saline, and eventually allowed to fill in and dry up, just like scab would.

I pictured the shaved pieces of skin made into a checkerboard, like dough made into latticework to fit over a pie. It sickened me that such a comparison came to mind, but Dr. Caruso said I had the right idea. "The right mechanics," he said.

I was there when he stopped by after rounds to tell Vincent they were on the operating room schedule.

"Now we get down to work, right?" Dr. Caruso said.

"Yes sir," Vincent said, all seriousness.

Dr. Caruso was a surgeon after all, and must have been eager to move from cutting away lifeless skin to the more positive work of laying on the healthy skin. "Grafts are precious," he said, "and fragile. You'll have to be careful. One little scrape and we could lose everything. Understand what I'm saying?"

"Yes, sir."

Dr. Caruso was looking rumpled and edgy. Vincent looked back at him, edgy too, behind his breakfast tray with its mess of dishes and spoon contraptions, cartons and straws poking out at various angles.

"How are you holding up, Mrs. Duvall?" Dr. Caruso asked, catching me off guard.

"I'm doing fine."

"Good." He strode away, passing the others on the ward — all that ruined flesh to take care of. As usual, the ties of his surgical gown were hanging loose at the back, revealing the khaki uniform underneath. He was a young man with far too much on his shoulders, but at the same time, at that moment, he seemed to me the most powerful doctor I would ever know. I didn't want to imagine how it would be to leave his care.

That day Father Smith came with Holy Communion for Vincent, accompanied by a corpsman serving as altar boy. Something about their whispering at the bedside reminded me of the day the old priest from St. Margaret's came to bring the last sacraments to my dying father. I recalled my mother lighting candles on the table in their bedroom, and how she held onto her little bottle of smelling salts while the priest was intoning his prayers, just as Father Smith was intoning them over Vincent. *May the blessing of God Almighty, Father, Son, and Holy Ghost, descend upon you and remain with you.*

Father Smith placed the host on Vincent's tongue. "The body of Christ."

Vincent kept his eyes closed.

Afterwards, I wished someone would turn on the radio. Across the room, Jimmy was asleep, his arm flung across a stack of comic books. Eddie and Mitch, two boys who had recently been moved to Vincent's side, were stretched out too.

"Is he gone?" Vincent murmured.

"Father Smith?"

"Yes. That guy gives me the willies."

"Vincent Duvall!" I said with a laugh. "Shame on you. And right after communion too."

In fact, there was something about Father Smith's manner — the lightness, the speed in getting away — that made me suspect he might have the willies himself.

I had a hand on Vincent's foot, which was half off the end of the mattress. The last time I'd bought him a pair of shoes, he'd worn a size eleven, and I was wondering if he'd stopped growing, those months of trudging around in Vietnam.

"What are thinking about, Mom?" he asked

"Oh, about what big feet you have."

He laughed pleasantly, and it seemed a good moment then to bring up what had happened the day he got so angry with me and called me a goddamned rock. But when I tried to bring it up, he brushed it off.

"Jeez, I don't remember half of that stuff," he said. "It's like the Sarge says — When it's the burn talking, you shouldn't pay attention."

"But I am the sort of person who's forever saying things will be all right," I said. "Sometimes it's important to rant and rave. I know there's a lot that isn't all right — things that shouldn't have happened, especially not to you."

"There's plenty of ranting and raving around here, Mom," he said matter-of-factly.

Jenks arrived at the bedside with a cart of water pitchers. "You got that right, Buddy," he said, collecting Vincent's pitcher and replacing it with a fresh one. "Ranting and raving, whining and complaining."

"And bitching and moaning," Vincent said.

"Vincent! I didn't raise you to talk like that," I said.

Both of them laughed. And I laughed too, but I think there was a lesson for me in it. There was only so much talking Vincent could handle with his mother. It wasn't necessarily a bad thing that he wanted to stand up to his troubles on his own.

Jenks jingled away with his cart of pitchers.

"Hey — Look who's here," Vincent said, nodding toward the doorway.

I looked, and there was Mary Kate, two steps behind Captain Garcia and then shooting past her, running toward Vincent, barely able to stop herself from throwing her arms around him.

"Well, well," she said breathlessly. "I see you're alive and lookin' good, Vinnie Duvall." She grabbed hold of the canvas bag on her shoulder and dropped it at his feet. Pinned to the flap of the bag was a peace symbol, a big button about the size of coaster. She had on a filmy peasant-looking dress — scoop neck, short puffy sleeves, dull-colored skirts. With her hair done up in pigtails, she looked like a girl of about 12 playing dress-up. She was wearing the same beat-up sandals I remembered from Easter Sunday.

Vincent was no more surprised at her entrance than he had been at Jack's. "I see you couldn't stay home and mind your own business," he said.

She laughed and looked around. Jenks was already swooping up a chair for her, carrying it across the room.

"Thanks," Mary Kate said, beaming up at him. "I'm his sister, Mary Kate."

"Alias Big Trouble," Vincent said.
Jenks beamed back. "I'm Jenks. But you can call me Paul."

17

When Vincent was four, he came down with a terrible case of the chickenpox. The spots popped up all over, even down into his little crotch. I was hard put to keep him occupied and not tearing himself up with scratching, particularly while the other two were at school. After breakfast, I'd bring him into my bedroom with his books and toys, where I could set up the ironing board, and try to get a little work done.

One day, I got out my button box. All the children loved that box, which was actually an old fruitcake tin with a Currier and Ives snow scene on top. It was filled to the top with buttons of every size, many of them old, handed down by my mother. I dumped the whole tin onto my bedspread, and Vincent dived into them with glee.

Another day, I dragged out a cardboard box of loose snapshots I hadn't put in the album yet. Vincent was soon bored with the pictures, but he rooted to the bottom of the box and found the three baby books I'd forgotten were in there. He wanted me to sit down and read the books to him. He was especially fascinated by Mary Kate's, which had a padded satin cover and charming illustrations.

Of course Mary Kate's book was carefully filled in on nearly every page: *first drink from a cup*, *first tooth*, *first haircut*, *first step*, *first birthday party*.

Jack's book didn't have nearly as many illustrations, but at least it was filled in, the entries short and sometimes scrawled in pencil.

Vincent's own book was the smallest. It had a yellow gingham fabric cover, with "Our Baby Boy" on the front. It was a gift from my neighbor Alma Henderson, who had written on the title page: "To Kitty, with love from Alma on the birth of Vincent Stephen Duvall." Unfortunately, after the *Measurements at Birth* page, and a few essential immunization dates, the pages weren't filled in at all.

Before Vincent could work up a protest, I declared I was awfully glad he'd found that book, since I'd been waiting for a nice quiet day when I could write in it with my good pen. I made a production about going downstairs to get the pen from the desk, and then filling it with ink from the bottle.

Vincent sat propped up against the pillows in my bed, content to watch me write in each of the blank spaces. I pretended to remember his infancy clearly, down to the exact day. A few of the events I actually did remember, if not the exact day, then at least the month, such as how he'd walked early, at 11 months, after being so late to crawl.

In many ways, the year Vincent turned four was best forgotten — sadness and turmoil, Frank gone off, who knew where, all the worries about how in the world I'd manage. But that time when Vincent had the chickenpox, that hour with the baby book — that I would always remember as something I'd done right.

❍

Like Jack, Mary Kate was friendly with all the patients on the ward. But more than Jack she made it her business to pay attention to the routine on the burn ward itself. Corpsmen, nurses, doctors — She recorded everything they did and said in the spiral notebook she carried in her bag.

"Jeez, what are you writing there, some kind of book?" Vincent asked.

She waved her hand and kept on scribbling.

It wouldn't have surprised me if Mary Kate were indeed writing a book. In college she'd majored in English, and she'd been writing poems since high school — strange, narrow poems that didn't rhyme and didn't use any punctuation. She was always trying to get published, and had actually succeeded a few times, in little journals I'd never heard of.

With Vincent, she was all positive energy, which was a good thing, since she'd arrived right when Vincent was scheduled for surgery.

She stayed at the guesthouse in my room, and the first night was awake until past midnight, talking and asking questions.

"So after the grafts, they'll discharge him, right?" she said. "From the Army, I mean. A medical discharge, right?"

"I guess so." It gave my heart a wrench to think that one day, sooner rather than later, they would indeed discharge Vincent from the Army, and then we'd have to leave Dr. Caruso and all the others, the ones who knew what was best for him.

"I'm pretty sure that's how they work it, Mom," she said. "They'll discharge him, and after that he'll be taken care of through the V.A."

"But we shouldn't be in a hurry for that." I got up on my elbow to look across the dark room at her. Lying there on the other bed in front of the window, with the lights of Fort Sam Houston beyond her, she looked so small, so child-like. "This is the right place for him now," I said. "They really know what they're doing here."

She had thrown me into a skid: All that worrying about the Army taking Vincent, and now I was facing the other way, worrying the Army would let him go.

"You're probably right," she said. "It's a research unit. They're probably testing out all kinds of new stuff."

Dog skin, I was thinking. Pig skin, the skin of real people, people who had just died. I recalled Dr. Caruso saying that Sulfamylon was fairly new. He hadn't called it an experiment, but the "best" they had.

"I can't believe I'm here," Mary Kate said dreamily.

"I can't believe it either," I said, lying back down. "You didn't have trouble getting time off at work?"

"Well jeez, they'd better let me take time off," she said sharply. "My brother was practically killed in Vietnam." After a moment she added, "Actually my boss was great about it."

"It was nice of your father to pay for the tickets," I said.

She turned onto to her side to face me. "I want you to know, Mom — I didn't ask Dad for the money. He offered. He said not to make a big deal out of it, because it was the least he could do."

"Your father calls a lot?"

"Every now and then. He feels bad about Vinnie."

There was a commotion outside the window, a helicopter circling closer, hovering. Mary Kate got up on her knees and looked out through the slats of the blind. "Looks like they're landing," she said. "Do you think it's a med-evac?"

"Maybe it's LBJ," I said.

"You're kidding. He comes here?"

"So they say. His ranch isn't far away. He comes to see the doctors."

"Wow," she said. "Good ol' LBJ. Wouldn't you just love to bump into him on the elevator? Wouldn't you just *love* to say 'Hey, President Johnson, come on down to the burn ward and meet the boys?'"

I heard the anger. I'd been wondering how long she'd manage it, how long before she'd veer into politics.

"I don't think it's likely you'll see him in the elevator," I said wearily, and thought twice about telling her the story of the peace symbol on the parking lot.

"Aren't you proud of me, Mom?" she said. "I'm being a good girl for you. No demonstrations on the lawn of Fort Sam Houston."

"Now that you mention it," I said. "It has been peaceful."

She laughed. "Well that's a good one, Mom. Pun intended?"

She turned away from me and was quiet for a long while. I thought she might have fallen asleep, but then she piped up one more time. "I can't believe it — all the way down here in Johnson Country . . . practically in Mexico."

The next morning, I woke at the crack of dawn, but Mary Kate slept so soundly I finally had to wake her up. We hurried over to the ward, and got there just as they were parking Vincent on the gurney in front of the nurses' station.

Mary Kate stood on one side, and I on the other, both of us trying to stay out of the way while Captain Garcia wrote some last-minute notes in his chart.

Ann Bukowsky called out from the medicine room. "Hello, Ladies! Come to give him the big send-off?"

"You bet," Mary Kate said perkily. But she looked less than perky, her hair needing work and circles under her eyes that I suspected were really mascara she'd missed washing off.

"I've got the biggest send-off of all," Ann said, arriving with the hypodermic needle. She leaned over Vincent and smiled. "Just a quick stick, O.K.?"

"You're the boss," he said.

"That's what you think." She flipped back the covers and administered the shot before he could work up a grimace. "There you go," she said, tucking him in again.

"Gee, thanks."

"Don't mention it." She was halfway back to the medicine room already.

"You know what I was thinking about last night, Mom?" Vincent said. "The button box — Remember how you used to let us play with it?"

"I remember," I said. "What was it about those buttons anyway?"

He licked his lips. "God, I'm dying of thirst . . . I don't know, I just remember playing with them."

"Remember those big flat buttons with the grooves?" Mary Kate said. "The ones that looked like little 78 records?"

Vincent laughed. "Yeah. They were cool."

My mother had cut those buttons off of a dress she'd worn back in the thirties. There had only been three or four of them, and Vincent would always tear through the pile, looking for them first.

"I used to think there were secret songs in those grooves," he said, "if only we could figure out how to play them."

The doors to the ward swung open and a corpsman in a surgical suit called, "Hello 14A! Y'all got somebody for me?"

"Right here," Captain Garcia said and handed him the chart.

He glanced through it quickly. "OK," he said, slipping the chart under the foot of the gurney. "We're going to take a little ride, Private First Class Duvall."

"See you later, Mom," Vincent said, as he was wheeled away. "Bye, Mary Kate."

I looked back through the doorway into the ward. They'd already made up his bed in preparation for his return — the pillow removed, the sheets pulled taut, the top covers folded regimentally to one side, the heat lamps in line with the I.V. pole. *First skin graft*, I was thinking.

"I don't know about you," Mary Kate said at my elbow, "but I need coffee."

We had coffee and doughnuts in the canteen, and returned to the waiting room, where we sat side by side on the tweed sofa that was beginning to feel so familiar I sometimes pictured myself reupholstering it.

Mary Kate had a book to read. I had some notepaper, and wrote two letters home, one to my mother and one to my sister. *They are doing Vincent's skin grafts today*, I wrote at the end of each letter. *It won't be long now before we come home*. It made me sick at heart to write about coming home — a homesickness for something I couldn't picture or even name.

At last Dr. Caruso arrived. Vincent had done fine, he said, everything had gone according to plan. Mary Kate asked a few questions, and wrote the answers in her notebook. Dr. Caruso said we should come back later, in the evening. "We need to keep him quiet, Mrs. Duvall. You understand."

He gave a professional smile and strode away.

"What now?" Mary Kate asked.

I suggested we take a walk.

The sun was high, the air hot and still. We crossed the circular island in the hospital parking lot, and at last I told my daughter about the peace symbol LBJ could probably see when he looked down from his helicopter, or from the windows of his suite at the top of the hospital.

I didn't get the reaction I expected. It almost seemed Mary Kate wasn't paying attention.

When we'd crossed the island — the peace symbol — she stopped and looked back. "My God," she said. "What terrible irony."

Out of the blue, she sat down on the grass.

I thought she might be feeling ill, but she said she was all right. I felt awkward standing over her like that, but I didn't want to sit down either. "Let's go back to the guesthouse, Sweetheart," I said. "It's too hot out here."

She didn't get up.

"Let's go, Sweetheart," I said, and held out my hand to her.

She took my hand and was getting to her feet, when a car pulled up and stopped — Hal, opening the door, coming towards us. "Isn't it a little hot for a picnic?" He smiled at Mary Kate. "I'm Hal Trainer. And you must Mary Kate."

"That's me," she said.

He turned to me. "How about I drive you ladies someplace for a bite to eat?"

It was Mary Kate who answered. "We'd love it," she said, already moving toward his car.

He took us to a restaurant called Genie's, a few blocks from the post. The dusty front window of Genie's was filled with browning ferns and disorderly spider-plants hanging from a curtain rod. When we stepped inside, the air-conditioning rushed over us, but the long and narrow room was crowded and hot-smelling — coffee, cigarettes, grease on a griddle. All the booths seemed to be taken.

A waitress balancing a loaded tray waved to us. She pointed to a table behind the last booth. "How you doing, Hal?" she called.

"I'm fine. How about you, Cissie?"

"Fine and dandy." She dealt the plates to a booth of boys with military haircuts. "Y'all need menus?" she called to us.

"The ladies will," Hal said.

We ordered sandwiches, and Hal said we should leave room for the apple pie. The sandwiches arrived in no time, accompanied by fat pickles and a mound of broken chips. I hadn't realized how hungry I was.

Genie's was noisy, and the boys with the military haircuts kept erupting in laughter. Meanwhile someone was feeding the jukebox — country songs, all of them sad and slow. It seemed someone in the room had a broken heart.

Hal and Mary Kate did most of the talking. Apparently he had once spent some time at Catholic University, and knew one of her favorite professors. He was interested in her job at *The Baltimore Sun*, and she was delighted to answer every question in detail. I was proud that she was so quick and smart, and also that she was polite, not a show-off.

For dessert we ordered the apple pie — a piece for Hal, and a piece that Mary Kate and I agreed to split. Just as Cissie was setting the plates on the table, Hal brought up the subject that made me nervous: the Catonsville Nine.

"I imagine that's been a big story in your neck of the woods," he said to Mary Kate, as he dug into the pie. "So what's the latest?"

She didn't bat an eye. "Not much," she said, putting her fork to the pie too. "Just a lot of speculation and rumor. The Berrigans are still underground."

"And Moylan?"

She glanced at him with a wry smile, her fork suspended. "I see you've been following the story pretty closely."

He nodded. "It's an interesting story — for clergy in particular."

"Did you know Moylan's a nurse?"

"I know. A nurse with a conscience."

She smiled knowingly, pleased with him, and in her element.

I took a bite of pie myself. It was very good, the crust as delicate as my mother's, the tart apples thinly sliced and piled high. I looked around the busy room, so noisy under that sad county song. I looked at Hal, and felt suddenly blue. When Cissie came with the check, I felt bluer still.

Afterwards, Hal drove us right to the door of the hospital, and we went back up to the ward, on the chance they'd let us in. There was no one at the desk to stop us, so Mary Kate and I washed up and put on our gowns.

We found Vincent sitting half-up in bed, one leg slung over the side. He was retching violently. There was a corpsman with him, a big fellow I'd never seen before. He had a washbasin under Vincent's chin.

My eyes were on the big strips of gauze on Vincent's thighs, moist and red, the blood oozing — the donor sites, where the good skin had been shaved away.

"Can you hold this?" the corpsman said to me, panic in his voice. "I'll go get the lieutenant."

"Stay here. I'll get her," I said, and took off running for the nurses' station myself.

I found Ann in the medicine room, and we ran back in time to see Vincent list sideways, banging his right arm hard against the bed rail. The corpsman grabbed the I.V. pole as it toppled. The washbasin hit the floor and spun around, clanging like an awful alarm bell, holding onto its little bit of vomit in the bottom.

"Watch the grafts," Ann said, reaching out for Vincent.

"No!" The wail came loudly behind us, and I turned to see Dr. Caruso come leaping across the room. He nearly knocked Ann over getting to Vincent — to Vincent's arms. He lifted those two arms in his hands like precious babies.

"What the hell's going on?" he said, glaring at Ann, while the corpsman hurriedly straightened Vincent's legs in the bed. "Can't you people read orders?"

"He was vomiting," Ann said.

"And you had to knock him around in the bed?"

"No sir."

The corpsman ducked down to retrieve the washbasin. It seemed to me he was the one who ought to be making the explanations.

"Are you all right?" Dr. Caruso asked Vincent.

"I'm O.K.," he said faintly. "Just sick to my stomach."

"He's had something for the nausea," Ann said. "I gave it an hour ago."

Dr. Caruso muttered something under his breath. He looked hard at Ann, and back at Vincent's arms. "I'll need the dressing cart. And a sterile tray."

"Yes, sir." She turned on her heel, and the corpsman followed.

In all this, Mary Kate and I stood to the side, frozen in our tracks. The rest of the ward was quiet, everyone watching the drama. Dr. Caruso didn't speak a word.

In a matter of seconds Ann was back with the cart, but without the corpsman. Dr. Caruso pulled on his mask. Ann pulled hers on too. Her hands were shaking, the plain gold wedding band lopsided and loose on her finger. Just a kid, I was thinking, and so much responsibility.

Ann unfolded the towel snappily from the surgical tray, and spread it open. She peeled back the paper from the gloves, so Dr. Caruso could shove his hands into them.

The dressing was removed from Vincent's hand. I let myself move a little closer, and I could see the grafts, white and shining against Vincent's red, raw flesh. They looked like gleaming little waffles, lined up side by side. Dr. Caruso had stretched that precious skin as far as it would go. It didn't make me sick to look. There was something beautiful about those shining pieces of skin, Vincent's own. They were a far cry from skin off a pig or a dog, or the graying skin of some poor soul who had died.

Dr. Caruso flexed his gloved fingers. "They're in place," he said. "They look O.K."

"I'm sorry," Vincent said.

"Just try to relax," Dr. Caruso said. He replaced the dressing carefully. "What about the pain? Do we have that under control?"

"It's not so bad."

"When's he due?" he asked Ann, stripping off his gloves and tossing them on the cart. He let his mask fall to his neck. He wasn't smiling.

"In an hour."

"Make sure he gets it on time." He turned and looked over his shoulder. "We need to keep him quiet, Mrs. Duvall. You and your daughter can come back in the morning, all right?"

That was the end of the positive energy Mary Kate arrived with. For the remainder of her visit — two more days — she brooded. Vincent was in pain from the grafts, thrown back into irritation and peevishness. He wouldn't eat for us, didn't want to talk much. There was nothing to keep Mary Kate on track. Mostly she stayed in the waiting room, writing in her notebook and staring at the people getting on and off the elevator.

She was out there the day Will Bishop appeared, and saw him get off the elevator and head for the burn ward.

"A man in a black hat," she told me later, "with these horrible scars on his face."

I was disappointed I'd missed Will. "He's a very nice person," I said. "There's something about him you can't help but like. I wish Vincent could meet him."

"I'd like to meet him myself," she said.

As luck would have it, she did meet Will. She was downstairs in the canteen, buying a candy bar, when he came in and struck up a conversation. He admired the enormous peace button on her bag, and the next thing she knew he invited her for a cup of coffee.

"You know, he has plans to go to law school," she told me.

"I didn't know," I said. "But I can picture it. He has a way about him."

"Charisma," she said, rooting in her bag. "He gave me this flyer." *Moratorium* was written prominently across the top. At the bottom Mary Kate had written some phone numbers. "He'll be in Washington in October. We might try to hook up."

Apparently they had made more immediate plans as well. That evening, just around the time I was getting ready for bed, Mary Kate was getting dressed to go out. Will and a friend of his were coming to pick her up. She wore the peasant dress, and took time to brush out her hair.

"You won't be late, will you?" I asked, because she would have to be up early the next day, to get to the airport in time.

"Yeah, I probably will." She laughed and hauled her bag to her shoulder. "But don't worry, Mom. You said yourself Will's a nice guy."

She didn't come in until after two in the morning, and fell right into bed, without even brushing her teeth.

"Did you have a nice time?" I whispered to her in the dark.

"A blast," she said.

18

I didn't think about it much back in 1969, but there was no comparing the war I lived through to the war Vincent lived through. My generation suffered, but we were all in it together. A schoolmate of mine from St. Margaret's, a sweet boy who'd once sent me a handmade valentine, was killed in his first jump on D-Day. My cousin Charles was killed not long after, and also the older brother of a girl I used to play with down the street. It was a very sad time for all of us. Frank Duvall — my high school sweetheart — went off to the Pacific on an aircraft carrier at the age of nineteen. I was crazy about him, and I knew there was a chance he might never come back, and yet there was little anger in my breast about it. There was only resignation, and determination to get through it, all of us together, so that we could get on with our lives.

Frank never spoke about the things he saw during the war. Once, in church, I saw him break down and cry over a hymn — *Eternal Father strong to save*, with that heartbreaking line, *Oh hear us when we cry to thee, for those in peril on the sea.* But he brushed me off when I tried to talk to him about it later.

He kept a box of papers in his dresser drawer, and in there was a clipping about an aircraft carrier that had gone down, a sister ship to his own. At one point or another in his leaving us, I noticed he'd taken that box with him, and I never saw it again.

❍

After Mary Kate went home, I knew it was time for me to go home too. I'd stayed almost three weeks. It seemed that Vincent had turned a corner, and he was embarrassed to have me hanging around, particularly as there were few other parents visiting. My walks around the post got longer, and my face and arms were getting very brown.

One day I walked down to the gate and found a small demonstration going on outside. A couple dozen protesters, some of them servicemen in ragtag military clothes, were walking back and forth with peace signs in front of the wrought-iron fence. I walked through the gate and slowly past them. They were a fairly orderly bunch, but when the military police arrived, they began to break up.

I wasn't watching where I was going. Suddenly someone backed into me, knocking me off balance, and I tripped off the curb onto my knees in the street.

A big, sweating fellow with a red bandana wrapped around his head muttered "Sorry." Someone else grabbed my elbow and righted me.

"Thank you," I said to no one in particular.

When I looked, it was Will Bishop peering down at me. He was wearing the black fedora, and carrying a black placard with a white peace symbol painted on it.

"Hello Will," I said.

He shook his head. "Really. We have to stop meeting like this."

I glanced at my knees. The right stocking was ripped, and the skin stinging.

"Are you all right?" he asked.

"I think so." I took a tissue from my pocket, and blotted at the blood on my knee.

"You got hit pretty hard," he said. "That guy must've weighed two fifty."

"I guess it was a pretty sight."

He chuckled. "Sorry. But it was kind of funny — You in your nice dress, doing that little dance off the curb. So — Did you come out to hear my speech?"

"You're making a speech?"

"Correction: I *made* a speech."

"Oh, I'm so sorry I missed it."

A friend appeared, a young man with long hair and a stringy mustache, who was wearing an Army shirt minus the sleeves. "We better get moving, Will," he said. "Looks like the party's over for now."

"Hey Chad," Will said. "This is Mrs. Duvall. Mary Kate's mom."

"You know Mary Kate?" I asked.

Chad smiled pleasantly, and shifted the duffel bag on his shoulder. "Yeah, we met the other night."

"You going up to BAMC, Mrs. Duvall?" Will asked. "It's hot as hell out here. We could give you a ride."

"If they let us," Chad said. "They're nervous at the gate right now."

"No problem," Will said. "They know me."

I followed them to a grimy little car, and climbed into the back seat. Chad shoved the peace sign and the duffel bag in beside me, and took the wheel. Will lowered himself into the passenger seat.

I took a good look at my knee then. The blood was oozing through the torn stocking, reminding me sadly of the mesh dressings on Vincent's donor sites. It was only a scrape, about a tenth the size of one donor site, and yet it was so painful.

"You better go the long way around to the other gate," Will said, removing his hat and placing it on the seat next to him.

I was stunned to see that he was almost entirely bald, and that nothing remained of his right ear but a little pink nubbin. When he stretched his arm across the seat I saw that his scars were white or silvery, not scabbed and bleeding like Vincent's. He and Chad were talking about people they'd seen at the demonstration, and about someone named Sheila, who hadn't shown up. Then they were talking about President Nixon. Chad spoke the name *Nixon* like something bad he had to spit from his mouth.

We arrived at the other gate.

"You live off-post now, Will?" I asked, as the military policeman waved us through.

"Yup. I have an apartment on Broadway."

"You have family here in San Antonio?"

"Nope. I'm a Yankee from New Hampshire. I'm just hanging out down here for a while."

"Hanging out and organizing demonstrations," Chad said.

Will laughed heartily. "Right on. Next gig, the White House."

"You're making a speech at The White House?" I said.

He turned around to smile at me in his distorted upside down way, revealing his lower teeth. "So to speak, in the general vicinity of the White House."

"Well, I'd like to hear that. I imagine you could make a very good speech."

"Thank you." He was still smiling. "So I take it you're with us, Mrs. Duvall?"

"I am."

I looked out the window at the face of Brooke Army Medical Center. It seemed it was burning itself into my heart.

"You can let me off at the guesthouse," I said.

"Sure," Will said, and directed Chad where to turn.

I leaned forward and dared to put a hand lightly on Will's arm.

"When you get to Washington," I said, "maybe you could come to my house for dinner. Mary Kate would like that. Washington isn't far from Baltimore, you know."

He nodded. "Thanks. I just might take you up on that."

"The man can really pack away the food, ma'am," Chad said. "You may regret that."

"Oh, I like it when people eat," I said. I dug in my pocketbook for the notepad, and scribbled the address and phone number quickly. "And you'd be welcome too, Chad, of course."

All of a sudden I really wanted to get back to my kitchen again, to that good feeling of setting a nice table and making sure everybody had enough to eat — to be like Martha in the gospel story, whose goodness was no less than her sister Mary's.

"There's a duffel bag back there, Mrs. Duvall," Will said. "Rustle in there and take one of my flyers. Maybe you can help us spread the word up in Baltimore."

I found the flyer in the bottom of the bag, under a couple of warm cans of beer and several articles of damp clothing. It was a Moratorium flyer, the one Mary Kate had shown me.

"Don't forget now," I said, getting out of the car. "I'll be expecting to see you in Baltimore. I'll bake you a pie. What kind do you like?"

"Pumpkin," Will said without hesitation.

"Yeah — I'd go for that too," Chad said.

"Pumpkin it is," I said, and leaned down to look in at the two of them through the window — the scarred young man with the red-rimmed eyes, and his young friend in the ripped and torn fatigues. "This isn't goodbye forever, right?"

"Not by a long shot," Will said. "Carry on now, Mrs. Duvall."

That afternoon, when I got up to the ward, I saw that Darby had someone new following him around: a second lieutenant named Paulson, a shapely blonde with her hair done up in a French roll.

Darby brought Lieutenant Paulson over to meet Vincent. Darby was in his glory explaining to her all of Vincent's exercises and the adjustments to the splints. As usual, he ignored me entirely.

"Let's see you bend this here," he said, pressing on Vincent's index finger. I saw a trickle of blood leak from one of the raw spots on the thumb and run right down into the dressings at the wrist. "Active, but assisted," he said, turning back to Lieutenant Paulson. "Otherwise you lose mobility faster than you think, because you've got these scars maturing, pulling against you. You can lose the tug of war real fast — contractures in every single joint — if you don't put the patient in charge." He pushed hard on Vincent's elbow. "Right, Vince?"

"Right." Vincent's face was screwed up with the pain, but he smiled for Lieutenant Paulson. She winced and smiled back. Her own pretty hands, with the nails perfectly manicured, were curled around the foot of the bed.

I'd had enough of that, so I wandered out to the nurses' station, where I saw Dr. Caruso.

"Looks like your son's getting himself into a normal routine," he said.

Normal routine. They were forever pushing for it. Vincent had to feed himself, brush his teeth, and even help with his own dressings. Only that morning, when he'd balked at the effort of pulling up his pants, Sergeant Berry had barked at him. *You got to be in control, son. You got to have a routine.*

"Yes," I said. "He's working hard."

"We're preparing for the boarding out process, you know. In a week or so he'll be discharged."

"Discharged from the hospital?" I asked.

"From the Army. It's standard procedure. After that, he'll be followed by the V.A."

"But I thought you were going to do more grafts."

"He's going to need a number of grafts, Mrs. Duvall. The surgeons at the V.A. can take over now."

"I'd rather you do it."

He smiled. "I wish I could see it all the way through to the end, but that's not the way it works. There're plenty of good surgeons in the V.A."

Only a few weeks ago it had seemed that the goal was to bring Vincent home, where he could laugh and joke at the dining room table the way he used to, and thump the basketball down the driveway, and practice his guitar. Now they really were packing him off to Baltimore, with the splints and the contraptions, and large areas on his arms and hands still not healed. It seemed too soon. It seemed careless somehow.

"You've done a good job here, Mrs. Duvall," he said. "But your son has a long road ahead. You ought to go home now and rest up. You know what we say in the Army — Conserve the fighting strength."

"You want me to leave now?"

He laughed. "Well not this afternoon. But as soon as you can comfortably make the arrangements."

"You took good care of Vincent," I said. "We're so grateful. I hope you take care yourself too. You're a very important person, you know."

"Thank you, Mrs. Duvall." He patted me on the shoulder, but I could see his mind was already moving on. Another stretcher was being pushed past us, another soldier coming back from the tank room.

I saw there was a little party going on in the nurses' station. Captain Garcia was handing out cups of soda and Sergeant Berry was cutting squares of sheet cake. When I got back to Vincent I asked him what the occasion was.

Vincent was digging into a piece of cake with his spoon contraption. "You didn't know?" he said. "It's Mike Darby's last day. He's going to Nam."

"That's awful," I said.

Vincent shrugged. "He's OK with it. He'll make captain while he's over there. He's career Army."

"But they should let him stay here. He's good at what he does. What will he do over there?"

"In a field hospital?" He rolled his eyes. "Don't worry — they'll find something for him to do."

Tears came to my eyes. Across the room, Darby's boyish face was a blur, as though he were already lost.

"Jeez, Mom," Vincent said. "Don't take it so hard."

Sergeant Berry came over with a piece of cake for me.

"You better watch out, soldier," he said to Vincent. "The new one's easy on the eyes, but don't kid yourself — Couple of days and she'll be just as mean as Darby. They train them well. You mark my words."

Vincent laughed. "I'm not worried. Another week and I'll be out of here."

"A week isn't very long," I said.

He groaned. "Around here it is."

"So it looks like I better get going myself," I said. "I'll have to get the house cleaned up before you come home."

He pretended to think it over. "I think that's a good idea, Mom."

I looked down at the cake on the paper plate — devil's food iced in white, with blue writing. I had the piece with the word *Good* and curl of the letter *L*.

In the next instant, a corpsman arrived to empty out Vincent's bedside stand. They were moving him downstairs to 13B. They were expecting a flight from Japan, the corpsman explained, and they needed Vincent's bed because someone had to come out of the Cube to make room for someone new coming in.

"Musical beds," Vincent said matter-of-factly.

"You got it," the corpsman said.

"How many on the flight?"

"Six."

Six more boys, I was thinking, six more mothers just getting the news, standing dumbstruck in the middle of the kitchen and wondering what to do first.

In a matter of minutes Vincent was escorted past the nurses' station, where the party was over now, and the usual pace had resumed.

Captain Garcia looked up from a chart and winked. "Toodaloo, Duvall, you handsome thing."

Vincent grinned and raised an arm like a politician in a parade. It wasn't as though he'd never see them again. He'd still be passing through on his way to the tank room.

I went back to the guesthouse, and called my brother-in-law Richard, to ask him to find out about the plane tickets home.

19

When Jack was in Cub Scouts, he made a three-dimensional map of the state of Maryland out of papier-mâché. Frank was around then, but he wasn't in very good shape. In the end, I was the one down in the basement, tearing the newspaper strips, making flour-and-water paste in the bucket, showing Jack how to mold the mountains that belonged in the west.

It was fall, close to Halloween, and so it was a busy time for me. I was also caught up in sewing a cowgirl costume for Mary Kate. One night, after the children were in bed, I went down to the basement to see if Jack's map was dry and ready to paint. I heard Frank come in, letting the screen door slam. He hadn't come home for dinner, hadn't even called. I heard him up there in the kitchen, probably looking around for something to eat. I stood there gazing at that mountain range, wondering if we ought to use white paint to represent a bit of snow on the tips.

Frank called me from the top of the steps. I could read him like a book by then, and so I knew he'd been drinking, and that he was angry about something.

I said I'd be right up, but he came stomping down after me anyway. He was angry because Mary Kate had left her bicycle out in the alley, and he'd knocked it over, parking the car. He said I was a lousy mother, a lousy housekeeper, a lousy wife. It was the wife part that hurt. He got right up in my face and hissed that I was nothing but a cold bitch.

I had a pain under the breastbone that frightened me. *Heartache* — I know why they named it that. It felt as though something in my chest had been stretched further than it ought to be, or were holding up under too much weight.

He stomped back upstairs. After a while I went up and found him asleep on the couch. That night I lay awake for hours, praying my rosary, and an old prayer that used to comfort me in those days: *Keep watch, dear Lord, with those who work or watch or weep this night, and give your angels charge over those who sleep. Tend to the sick ones, bless the dying ones . . .*

❍

There was a note on my door: *Ann Bukowsky called.*

I telephoned the ward at once.

"Hi, Mrs. Duvall," Captain Garcia answered in her chipper way. "How ya doin'?"

But when I asked to speak to Lieutenant Bukowsky, there was an odd pause. "She's not here right now," she said, less chipper. "Can I help you?"

"Someone left a note that she called."

"Can you hold on a minute?" She put the phone down, and I could hear her talking to someone else.

Then Colonel Anderson got on. "About what time did Lieutenant Bukowsky call, Mrs. Duvall?" she asked. "We're a little concerned here. She was supposed to be here at three o'clock."

"I don't know," I said.

"Well, if she calls again, would you have her contact me? Just to set my mind at ease?"

As usual, the evening stretched before me with nothing much to do. I picked up a newspaper from the parlor and carried it outside, where there was a bench in the shade of a live oak tree.

Kissinger details Vietnamization. I didn't know what *Vietnamization* meant, but it hardly mattered any more. *Copter Shot Down Near Danang, 10 Killed.*

I turned the front page on its face and pulled out the society pages, but the reading there wasn't particularly safe either — weddings and engagements, photographs of brides in various poses and finery. I could only think of Pete saying *fiancé* with such pride, and of Caroline, weeping on the other side of the wall, and later heading back to Austin in Pete's Mustang.

An ad at the bottom caught my eye. *Mothers Take Heart!* At the Brittany Buffet you could get the shopper's special, meat and two vegetables — *Relief from all that back-to-school shopping!*

Back to school: I'd already called Sister Regina, the principal at St. Anthony's, to say I wouldn't be back to work until after Vincent came home. She had crooned in her Irish brogue that all the sisters were praying for him. "Take care of yourself too, Kitty dear."

In the yard of the enlisted family across the road, a little girl was flying back and forth on the swing set. On the lawn of the guesthouse, two young men in bare feet were tossing a Frisbee back and forth, boys right out of college probably, newly commissioned officers. I'd just folded up the paper when I saw a white car come slowly up the main road, circle in front of the hospital, and turn down the side street. A minute later it reappeared, following the same route, a slow circle in front of the hospital. It was the same car — battered, with a stripe of rust along the side — that I'd seen Ann's husband leaning against, when he was staring up at the hospital that day.

The third time around, the car came to a stop in front of the guesthouse. The driver's door opened, and there was Ann in her white uniform, wobbling around the front of the car, and then sitting abruptly down on the sidewalk.

I ran to her across the lawn, and so did two the two young men with the Frisbee.

"Are you all right?" the one young man said.

"Are you sick, Ann?" I took hold of her hand. It felt dry and cold.

"Just a little faint," she said.

"I'll call the M.P.'s," the other young man said. "You need a doctor."

"No," she cried. "Please. I'm all right now."

"She doesn't look all right to me." The one squatting on the curb swiveled around to look up at me, and then at his friend, who nodded in agreement.

We helped her to her feet.

The circles under Ann's eyes were pronounced in her pale face. I took her arm, as she walked slowly toward the guesthouse, and the two young men followed. They went inside with us, as far as my room, where they filled the doorway with their hovering concern.

"You sure you don't want a doctor?" the one asked.

"No," Ann said emphatically. The hat was off-kilter on her head. She stood precariously in the center of the room, as though the starched uniform alone were holding her upright.

The young men shrugged, and left us alone.

"Maybe you're overheated," I said. "Let's at least take off your hat."

She removed the bobby pins and handed me the hat. "I've got to lie down," she said.

"Why don't you slip out of that hot uniform first?" I said.

She let me help her with the buttons down the front. After the uniform had dropped on the floor, she sat down stiffly on the edge of the bed in her slip. I flung her uniform over the chair, and then I got down in front of her and quickly untied her nurses' shoes, which were chalky white, newly polished, ready for duty. Such a hot day, and yet her feet were as cold as her hands.

I pulled back the bedspread and she lay down and faced the wall, her knees curled against her chest. Through the thin slip, I could see the knobs of her spine and the sharp curve of her hipbone.

"Colonel Anderson is worried about you," I said, pulling the sheet over her. "I'm going to go out and call her now. Just to let her know you're all right."

"Please," she said. "Don't do that."

I sat beside her on the bed. "What is it?" I asked. "Is it your husband? Did something happen?"

"He didn't hit me, if that's what you mean." Her voice was muffled, her face buried in the pillow. "He's never hit me."

"All right. But what happened then?"

"He threw a plate against the wall, and it broke, and there was spaghetti all over the rug." The words were choked, broken with sobs. "I was trying to clean it up. I was trying . . . He kept calling me horrible names . . ."

The story writhed back and forth, and half the time I could barely make out what she was saying. "He didn't mean any of it," she said, wiping her eyes, turning to really look at me for the first time. "It's like a demon has hold of him. Ever since he came back from Vietnam. Tomorrow he'll take it all back, and things will be fine."

"Of course he didn't mean it." I believed that. Still, there was something in the story I recognized all too well — that helplessness in the face of someone else's fall, that refusal to let go. I saw myself at the same age, crying over some drunken cruelty of Frank's, putting on the happy face for the sake of the children. My heart was full of pity. I didn't know what to do with it. And then I thought of Hal.

"I'm going to call the chaplain," I said. "It would be good for you to talk to him."

"Please don't do that," she said into the pillow.

"I'm sorry," I said, already heading for the phone. "We've got to do something, and I can't think of anything else."

Miraculously, it was Hal who answered the phone in the chaplain's office. "Uh-oh," he said, when I told him Ann was there with me. "I hear the kid's AWOL."

"AWOL?" I knew what that meant — absent without leave, something that could get you picked up by the military police, maybe even thrown in jail. Ann had been so frightened — Had I just turned her in?

He laughed. "Relax. I'm kidding. Do you want me to come over?"

"Yes. You'd better come."

I went back to the room and told Ann he was coming. She threw the covers off. "He's coming here?"

I went to the closet for my robe, and helped her slip it on. I ran a glass of water in the bathroom, and opened up the tin of butter cookies, a gift Barbara had brought.

But she only shook her head, and lay down again, closing her eyes.

I watched out the window for Hal. It appeared Ann had fallen asleep. What was Vincent doing at the moment, I wondered, and how had it come about that I was drifting away on this other sad drama? When I saw Hal striding across the lawn, I hurried out to meet him.

We returned together and found Ann standing in the doorway to the bathroom.

"Hello, Hal," she said softly, and then it seemed something vital gave way, and she dropped in front of us, right to the floor, with more weight than it seemed she had on her bones.

Hal leaped forward, but not in time. Her head struck the sink on the way down. She hit the floor like a doll with the rubber band snapped, a doll dressed up in my seersucker bathrobe. And then she was very still. I saw Hal lift her wrist, and realized he was taking her pulse. I saw him lift her head, the blood pooling in his hand.

I took off running for the phone in the hall, praying *Please, God, please.*

The rest was a blur — the young corpsmen lifting Ann tenderly onto the stretcher, the whirling lights of the ambulance, the curious ones murmuring their way back into the guesthouse, and the two young men looking at me as if to say *We told you she needed a doctor.*

It was long past midnight when Hal called. A few stitches to the scalp, he said, and nothing broken. And yet they'd admitted her — to a ward in Beach Pavilion, that building with an old-fashioned, southern-sounding name, reminding me of a sanitarium, a place where the patients would sit outside in their bathrobes on sunny porches.

But apparently they took care of serious illnesses in Beach Pavilion, because Hal said Ann was very seriously ill. "She's been starving herself," he said. "They had to give her fluids." There was an angry edge to his voice. "The doc said it was a miracle her heart didn't go haywire. Her electrolytes were all screwed up. People can die from this sort of thing."

But before I could ask a question, he cut me off. "She's OK now," he said. "Jeannette Anderson's with her. You get some sleep."

20

The day after Vincent left for Vietnam, I thought I'd do a little shopping in Hutzler's department store downtown. Christmas was coming, and I hadn't done a thing to get ready. It was important that I stay on track, and keep myself busy.

It was a clear day, but cold and windy. I walked up to Belair Road and was standing at the curb, watching for the bus, when a girl arrived and stood next to me. She was wearing a skimpy skirt and a short jacket, and I was thinking her legs must have been awfully cold. But of course she was the height of the fashion, whereas I was bundled up in the same brown coat I'd worn to my father's funeral, fifteen years earlier.

She had a transistor radio with her, and began to fiddle with it.

For the times, they are a-changing. Bob Dylan — I remembered that Vincent had bought that very same record for Mary Kate's birthday.

I stood beside that girl, listening to her little radio, and it struck me then that the songs on the radio wielded a lot of power over the young, maybe more power than the television ever had. An entire generation carried away on the radio waves, I was thinking.

Of course I preferred the music of my own generation — the Andrews Sisters in the forties, and on into the Lennon Sisters on the Lawrence Welk Show — and for a long while I didn't pay much attention to those protest songs. But standing at the bus stop that cold day, one phrase coming out of that girl's radio hit me hard: *It'll soon shake your windows and rattle your walls.* That man was wailing his song right at me, and in my mind's eye I saw our house on Constance Avenue shaken, all that I held dear falling, along with everything else Vincent was supposed to be fighting for.

❍

Sunday again — my last visit to the Fort Sam Houston Chapel — and when I came out after Mass, I found Hal waiting for me at the curb beside his car. He smiled, but he looked rather serious in his dark green uniform and hat.

"Ah, the faithful Catholics," he said. "It's easy to find them on Sundays."

"You're dressed up," I said. "No tennis today?"

"Ouch," he said, and opened the car door. He took off his jacket and hat, and tossed them in the back. "I came to give you a report on our friend Ann. And a ride, if you'd like."

I got in the car, my heart sinking at how glad I was to see him, and how familiar his car was beginning to feel.

"Well the good news," he said, once we were on our way, "is that she's looking better this morning. She's still hooked up to IV's, but her condition is stable."

I was relieved, and thanked him for coming to let me know.

We were passing the commissary, then the P.X. In the distance the barracks were lined up far and away, like blocks a child had arranged in the dirt. I rolled down the window and let the air rush over my face. I was feeling disoriented again, and tried to call up the home I'd be going back to — the houses across the street on Constance Avenue, Alma Henderson's hedges trimmed into the shape of little castle turrets.

"She asked me to thank you," he said. "I've got your bathrobe, by the way — It's on the back seat. The nurses washed it, so it's still a little damp."

I glanced over my shoulder, and saw the bathrobe, which had fallen partly out of a paper bag. It gave me a start to see the arm of his jacket flung over it like that.

"Did you get to talk to her?" I asked.

"A little. The husband was with her. Poor kid, scared to death."

We were approaching the old Quadrangle, passing into the shade of the taller trees. I thought of the deer and the peacocks on the other side of the wall. I thought of Caroline, that day we drove off post. But Caroline was gone now, and Pete was dead, and now there was Ann to think about, and the angry husband who hadn't been right since he came back from Vietnam. *For better or worse, in sickness and in health, until death do us part.* I was remembering the little knobs along Ann's spine, the sharpness of her hipbone, the dark circles under her eyes. *People can die from this sort of thing.*

"About Ann's husband," I said. "I think he takes it out on her."

He kept his eyes on the road. "Did she tell you that?" he asked evenly. "Did she say he abused her?"

"She said he never hit her."

"It doesn't have to be hitting, you know."

I knew.

I looked at Hal's hands on the wheel — square and tanned, the blond hair on the knuckles. I pictured him gripping his prayer book by the spine, swinging it along as he strode through the ward. And then, remembering how he had held Ann in his arms after she fell, I was overwhelmed with longing to be comforted myself.

"Maybe you don't want to talk to me about it, Kitty," he said. "If you're not comfortable, we could get someone else. Jeannette Anderson would be good."

"It's not that," I said quickly. "I'm a little upset, that's all. Really, there isn't much to tell."

He glanced over, arching an eyebrow. "If you're upset, I imagine there is something to tell. Was she asking you for help?"

"I think maybe she was."

"Is it drugs?"

"She didn't say. But she's frightened. I sense there's more to it than a plate of spaghetti hitting the wall."

"He threw a plate at her?"

"At the wall. That's what she said."

"All right. I'll get Jeannette to talk to her. Jeannette will get to the bottom of it. And that way we stick to the proper chain of command." He turned to look at me. "Are you comfortable with that?"

"Yes."

We were passing through the gate, the M.P. saluting snappily.

"I didn't even have time for a cup of coffee this morning," he said. "How about you? Are you hungry?"

"I didn't have time either."

"We could go down to the Riverwalk. If you come to San Antonio, you have to see the river."

I hesitated.

"It's early yet," he said leaning forward to ease into traffic, to look past me past me with his intense blue eyes. "We can get something quick, and I'll have you back in a jiffy."

The farther we went toward the heart of the city, the slower traffic was moving. Cars were parked tight all along the streets, and the sidewalks were filling with people in their Sunday best. An altar boy ran along the curb, carrying his robe and surplice on a hanger. Two little girls twirled past in what looked like First Communion dresses. But it was not May, the month for First Communions. It was a hot August Sunday in San Antonio, Texas.

"I don't know what this traffic is all about," Hal said. "Something going on at the Cathedral, I guess. Oh wait, I do know. Damn — It must be the Archbishop."

I laughed. "Damn?"

"I kid you not — They're installing the new Archbishop today. We better stay away from the Cathedral. It'll be a mess."

An Air Force officer in dress uniform strode past on the sidewalk, moving faster than the cars. "See that?" Hal said. "They'll have representatives from every military base in town. It's a very big deal. Lots of dignitaries and a long procession, I bet."

When we were stopped at a light, I saw a boy holding his little sister by the hand while their father lifted a basket of paper garlands from the trunk of the car. The children were dressed in fancy Mexican clothes, both of them in yellow and black. The girl's dark hair was fastened with flowers like those in the basket. Suddenly she pulled away from her brother and held out the yards of her ruffled skirt, her dangling earrings catching the light. It was such a pretty sight that it made me sad.

"I went into the Cathedral the other day," I said. "I took a bus — that rainy day, when I was all upset about Vincent yelling at me."

He turned to look at me. "You picked a good place to go."

"I left my rosary there," I said. "Actually, I think it might have been Vincent's rosary once upon a time, his First Communion rosary — not that he ever used it. I found it in the bottom of his drawer at home."

"And you left it at the cathedral?"

"Yes. At the feet of the Blessed Mother."

"Ah," he said, nodding. "That's really something, isn't it? — all those petitions, and photographs."

He found a place to park, close to a stairwell leading down to the river. It was good to get out of the car. I was damp with perspiration, and had to shake my skirt from the backs of my legs. There was a little breeze rising up the stairs, and mariachi music.

"By the way," he said, plopping his hat on his head, not bothering to pull the brim straight and serious over the eyes, the way most military types did, "where's your hat? The one with the cherries?"

"It didn't quite go with the outfit."

"Really? I like that hat."

He took me by the elbow and led me down the stairs to the riverwalk. There was a small restaurant down there, tables outside in the open air. A girl in a halter dress seated us at a table near a low wall. Three steps down was the San Antonio River, a narrow channel of gray-green water — Army-green, slow moving. Along the other side, which could be reached in a few steps over the footbridge, a path wound as the river wound, and disappeared at the bend. There were strings of electric lights looped between the old cypress trees. I imagined it would be even prettier at night.

It was early, but we ordered from the lunch menu anyway — iced tea and sandwiches with fancy names, an "Alamo Platter" and an "El Chaparral." Then we sat watching the flat boats that appeared now and then from under the stone bridge, some of them set up like floating restaurants, with waiters busily weaving among tables draped with pastel cloths, preparing for lunch. I felt as though I'd seen it all before, or at least a drawing of it, in a picture book I'd read to the children long ago, or maybe in a book I'd read as a child myself — a river in a fairy tale, a beautiful hidden river, running below the city.

"I guess this is what you call getting away from it all," I said, meaning away from the burn ward, but it also occurred to me how far off home was, in more ways than the miles. "You'd think I'd be homesick by now, but I'm not. It's strange."

"Not so strange," Hal said. "You've been thrown violently out of your everyday life. You haven't had time to look over your shoulder."

We both looked to the river then, at another boat going by. It was comfortable to be sitting across from him, to say nothing.

"So when do you leave?" he asked.

"Day after tomorrow. In the afternoon."

He pressed his lips together and nodded thoughtfully. "I'll probably be here a couple more months myself. But I've decided to resign my commission. I'm getting out."

"Why?" I asked, though I already knew.

"They're all so young, Kitty," he said. "Too many dying, for no good reason I can see anymore."

I tried to imagine what it would be like to resign a commission, or rather what it would be like to decide to resign one. There was nothing comparable in my own life. Even taking off for San Antonio to be with Vincent — a real effort, my first time to travel any distance from home, my first time to fly — hadn't been much of a decision, but just something I knew I had to do, a given. A war I didn't understand had caught us up, and my job was to get on the plane, simply because

I was the mother. I had no thought at the time for what I'd do when the plane landed.

"Where will you go?" I asked.

"I'm still working that one out."

On the next boat to float by, a mariachi band was performing. The singer with the drooping mustache looked right at me, threw his head back, and let the guitar fall against his ruffled blouse. *Guadalajara, Guadalajara* — He sang right at me, as though to deliberately hurt me. Beyond him, all of San Antonio seemed cruelly bright, beautifully sad — the music, the colors, the winding river and the tall gleaming building beyond the trees.

"Well, at least you won't be leaving right away," I said, and smiled at him. His strong, clean-shaven jaw, his expressive mouth — Surely he knew how attractive he was. Surely there was a woman in his life.

He leaned forward, enough that I felt the difference. "If you want, we could exchange addresses, so we can stay in touch."

I said I'd like that. He leaned back then, apparently satisfied we'd settled it.

Our sandwiches arrived, and he changed the subject, quizzing me playfully about the Baltimore Orioles, asking if I thought they'd take the pennant. I admitted that I didn't pay that much attention to baseball, though my mother was a big fan who listened to all the games on the radio.

"And the Colts? Does your mother like the Colts?" he asked.

"No, only baseball for her."

"Vincent tells me he played basketball in high school."

So I ended up telling him the whole story, even the bad part about Vincent getting kicked off the team for hiding the beer on the bus. I told him how it felt to be sitting in the bleachers back in those basketball days, too thrilled to even yell with the rest of the crowd, as Vincent dribbled fast toward the basket.

"Maybe playing ball would be good therapy for him a little further down the road," he said.

"Maybe it would." I was so happy then, just to picture it.

As Hal had promised, it wasn't long before we were heading back in the car. A few blocks from the restaurant, as we were passing through an intersection crowded with tourists, I saw a small, very old building, crammed in among the modern buildings. It took me a moment to realize it was the Alamo, because it looked unreal, like a huge cardboard replica of itself.

"Is that really the Alamo?" I said.

He laughed. "A lot of people have that reaction."

"I always pictured it out in the open, with sage brush all around."

"We'd have to drive pretty far out of town to find sagebrush."

It was a pleasant thought — riding through miles of sagebrush with him, riding on, out to the hill country, far away. I wrenched myself from it. "I guess we'll be back in time for the lunch trays," I said.

"You bet."

And we were, but it didn't really matter. The pretty new girl, Lieutenant Paulson, was working with Vincent, and he seemed embarrassed to have me around. I let him off the hook, and said I had things to do at the guesthouse.

"Hey, Mom," Vincent said, as I was turning to go. "Did you hear about Lieutenant Bukowsky?"

Of course he'd heard the news. The burn ward was small. "Yes," I said evenly. "I did hear."

"It's too bad. She was a real good nurse."

I was startled he put it in the past tense, and so matter-of-factly, as though it were understood we'd never see Lieutenant Ann Bukowsky flitting nervously around the ward again.

21

Once, moving things around in the attic, I jostled a box of old books and out fell a catechism. It was covered in brown paper, the way the nuns at St. Anthony's insisted every schoolbook be covered, and Vincent had printed his name on it in the right hand corner. Under his name he had doodled a little dog with a smiling face.

I carried the catechism downstairs with me, and later in the day sat down to have a look.

Who made you?

God made me.

Why did God make you?

As a girl I'd memorized the same questions and answers.

I flipped idly through the chapters, and by accident came to Lesson 35 — "Matrimony" — Question 462: *Why has the Catholic Church alone the right to make laws regulating the marriages of baptized person?*

Because the Church alone has the authority over the sacraments and over sacred matters affecting baptized persons.

The words went in a circle, not really explaining why the Church alone had the right. But ever since childhood I'd understood: Even though Frank had abandoned me, and not the other way around, I would never be free to marry another, at least not in the eyes of the Church. Catholics who broke the laws regulating marriage would be set free indeed, to do as they pleased, because they would be excommunicated, cut off from the beloved sacraments, cut clean forever from the Holy Mother Church.

❍

I couldn't stop thinking about Hal. On Monday morning — the day before I was to leave Fort Sam Houston — I was out walking as soon as the sun was up.

I recalled every moment I'd spent with him, from the day I first saw him striding toward me, whistling that happy tune. *A silly crush*, I told myself, and it would pass, as soon as I got home.

Impulsively, I decided to take the bus to the cathedral, to pray there one more time, to lay all my worries at the feet of the Blessed Mother.

When the bus rode over the river, I thought I saw the place where Hal had parked the car, and the stairs going down to the little restaurant. I pulled the cord, my heart lurching as the bus lurched to a stop. But after I got off, I realized it wasn't the right set of stairs after all, because there was no restaurant at the bottom.

When I made it to the cathedral, the early Mass was just beginning. I took a pew near the statue of the Blessed Mother, and saw that Vincent's rosary was right where I'd left it. The photograph of the baby Rosemarie was gone, but there was a new photograph resting against the feet of the Mother — a smiling soldier in fatigues, so baby-faced he might have been a kid playing in the back yard, dressed up like GI Joe.

I tried to concentrate on the Mass, but again it was Hal on my mind, and my heart beat fast, angrily, as though a cruel joke had been played on me. I was sealed off from love and tenderness, banished from it. And who was to blame for that? The husband who left me? The Holy Mother Church?

After Mass, the priest announced he would hear confessions. I watched him genuflect and go around to the side aisle to the confessional. The door clicked shut, a few people left their pews to get in line, and I got in line behind them.

When I entered the confessional, I closed my eyes in the darkness behind the curtain, and tried to run through the *Memorare* in my head, so as not to hear someone else's sins being told on the other side. Too quickly the door slid open.

"Bless me, Father, for I have sinned," I began. "It's been a month since my last confession." I paused to steel myself, and could hear his breathing from the other side of the screen.

"Go on, my child," he whispered, shifting closer, his ear directly in front of my mouth.

"I've been having thoughts about another man." It was a relief to let it out.

"You're married?"

"Yes. But my husband and I are separated. He left me years ago."

"Mere thoughts are not always sinful in themselves. Do you act upon these thoughts? Do you deliberately put yourself in the path of temptation?"

"Not deliberately."

"You understand that it would be a grave sin to knowingly allow an occasion of sin?"

"Yes, Father."

"And do you recall that the chief means of preserving purity are prayers to the Blessed Mother?"

"Yes, Father."

"Good. Are there any other sins you wish to confess?"

"No."

"Concern yourself with keeping your marriage vow, my child. Pray to the Blessed Mother. There's a special place in her heart for you. Do you pray the rosary regularly?"

"Yes, Father."

"Good. And also frequent Holy Communion, of course. For your penance, say five decades of the rosary. May God bless you." He raised his hand in the sign of the cross and slid the screen shut before I could finish blessing myself.

I pulled back the curtain, and walked down the aisle and out. The first thing I saw, when my eyes adjusted to the sunlight, was a hearse parked at the curb and two men in dark suits — undertakers — standing by front fender. *Until death do us part.* And there it was again, that wish that Frank would set me free in the only way he could, that he would drop painlessly and absolutely dead.

I went back inside, up the aisle, and got in line behind the one remaining person. When it was my turn again, and the screen slid open, I didn't bother with the usual. "Father," I said outright, "I was in here a few minutes ago, and there was something important I didn't say."

"You wish to make another confession?"

"No. It's just a question."

"Yes?"

"I understand that you have to keep a vow. But it was my husband who left, not me. I've been alone so long. How can I love and honor someone who isn't there? He's made it impossible for me to keep my vow."

He seemed to adjust himself on the other side of the screen. "It is not impossible to keep yourself pure, my dear." His tone was flat and cold. "When you married at the altar of God, you gave yourself to one man alone."

"I have so much anger in my heart over this," I said.

"Have you considered an annulment? It's possible the marriage could be declared invalid. If you call the rectory, someone could put you in touch with the diocesan tribunal."

I wanted to pound my fists against the screen. How could we ask for an annulment, when it wasn't as though either Frank or I had lied at the altar, or as though the marriage had never been consummated? Those were the only grounds for annulment, as far as I knew.

I got up from my knees then, and went out through that heavy curtain.

As I headed for the bus stop, I looked over my shoulder at the San Fernando Cathedral. I was angry at the priest, at the unfairness. But at the same time, I could have wept at the countenance of that old church, for I knew I wouldn't be back again.

On the way back to Vincent, I decided to stop at Beach Pavilion and pay a quick visit to Ann. I found a small crowd gathered outside the building. Four important-looking cars were parked at the curb, and a couple of military policemen were stationed near the entrance.

"What's going on?" I asked a woman with a camera around her neck.

"It's the new Archbishop," she said. "The commanding general just took him inside."

"I guess that's a big news," I said.

"Oh yes, very big. You should have seen the ceremony at the cathedral on Sunday. It was gorgeous. All these beautiful Mexican costumes."

"Is he Mexican?"

She gave me an odd look. "No."

Inside, I found Ann sitting in the sunroom, wearing a hospital bathrobe and bright pink lipstick that made her complexion looked more washed-out than ever. Her hair was combed severely back, revealing a bald spot above the left ear, where the hair had been shaved away and there was a tidy row of black stitches.

"Hi, Mrs. Duvall!" she cried cheerily from the edge of the chair, looking like any second she might slip onto the floor.

The conversation got off to a strained start. I asked the usual hospital-visit questions. *Is the food good? Can you sleep at night?* Ann gave the usual short answers. She didn't seem to perk up until it was her turn to ask the questions. She asked about Vincent's grafts. She asked about each of the boys on Vincent's side of the room. "I guess Jimmy was discharged," she said.

"Yes. He left his comic books to Vincent."

She laughed. "What a little sweetheart."

We ran out of the things to talk about. I gazed out at the traffic in the corridor, at a man pushing a younger man in a wheelchair — father and son, I was sure of it because they looked so much alike — and then a woman walking arm in arm with a boy in a hospital bathrobe just like Ann's. "Straighten up, Charlie. Come on, honey." The boy tried to square his shoulders. His broad, childish face was creased in pain.

How far from home had those people traveled to be with their boys? All of us at Fort Sam Houston, both the sick and the able-bodied, were only passing through.

"Well," Ann said. "Will you tell everybody I said hello?"

It sounded more like goodbye, and I knew then that Vincent had been right: She wouldn't be going back to the burn ward. I wondered if they would put her out of the Army altogether. *Hurry up and wait.* That's what they say about military life, but it was only the hurry-up part that I experienced at Brooke Army Medical Center, where people moved dramatically into my life and dramatically out with awful speed.

"I've been worried," I said, "after what you told me about your husband the other night."

She pulled the bathrobe tighter across her chest. "You don't have to worry, Mrs. Duvall. Colonel Anderson has arranged for me to take a leave. I'm going home tomorrow, to visit my parents for a while."

"By yourself?"

"Yes."

I got out my notepad and pencil. "Maybe you could write down your parents' address for me. I'd like to stay in touch."

While she was writing, I looked up and saw that her husband had come. He was hanging back at the threshold of the sunroom, a bouquet of flowers in one hand and a pink envelope in the other. Ann waved to him, but still he hung back.

"Goodbye, Ann," I said. "Take good care of yourself, now."

"Goodbye, Mrs. Duvall." She wasn't looking at me. Her troubled eyes were on her husband. The husband nodded politely as I passed, but he didn't look me in the eye either.

People moving into my life, and people moving out — It went on even into my last evening in Fort Sam Houston. When I got back to the guesthouse at the end of the day, prepared to pack my suitcase, I saw the new parents, Betty and Tom Crenshaw, sitting in the parlor. I'd introduced myself to them earlier, when they first arrived, Betty in the pink shirtdress with the packing creases running down the skirt, Tom with the shaving nick on his chin, both of them looking frightened behind their quick hellos.

I went over and sat down with them, to see how they were doing. Betty was a big talker. She went on and on about their son Albert, how he'd graduated magna cum laude from Rutgers University, and how there was a good job waiting for him, because he knew everything there was to know about the big computer on campus. Tom had little to say, but whenever I smiled at him, he blinked and smiled back hard.

Betty didn't say anything specific about Albert's burns until I asked.

"They said the burns are eighty per cent," she said.

I tried not to let the enormity of it show in my face. "It will be hard," I said. "But the doctors and nurses are wonderful here. This is probably the best place in the whole world, if you have burns."

"Eighty per cent," Betty said again, slowly, as though something had tripped her and now she needed to go back and look it over. Suddenly, she curled herself against Tom's shirtfront and burst into tears.

I thought of my own son, with one set of grafts behind him already. But I knew better than to offer that up as hope to Betty Crenshaw. Vincent's number was thirty-six. A far cry, I was thinking, a far cry.

"Can I get you anything?" I asked, when she seemed to get control of herself. "Something to drink, maybe?"

She shook her head. Tom looked stricken.

"My room's at the end of the hall," I said, and got to my feet. "If there's anything I can do."

But there was nothing to be done really, except pray, and once again it struck me how nearly unbearable it was to be somebody's mother on the burn ward, and to stand there, stunned and helpless, while the doctors and nurses and corpsmen ran around in circles, doing important things that actually made a difference.

Albert Crenshaw was dying. I'd said the right things, the kind and supportive things. It was all I could do then to leave them, each step separating me that much farther from the sorrow that might have been mine.

I was heading for my room when Hal came into the guesthouse, looking for me.

"Can we step outside," he said, and I followed him out into the warm evening air.

"I thought you ought to know," he said. "We just got some terrible news. Ann Bukowsky's husband is dead. He committed suicide this afternoon."

I was speechless, picturing that boy I'd seen only hours before, that boy on the threshold of the sunroom, clutching his flowers and the card in the pink envelope. How could he turn around and do such a thing? *Phil's a good person. Right now he's hurt.*

"Come on — let's walk a little," Hal said.

He walked fast, and talked fast too, sorting through what little we both knew about Ann and her husband, as though he were looking for some place to lay the blame. At first he was saying the Army was too big, that people could get lost in the system. Then he was saying that his own unit was so small, and yes, they were overwhelmed with trauma, but wouldn't you think someone would have picked up on it, if Ann were having that much trouble with the poor kid, at least before it got so bad he put a gun to his head?

"He shot himself?" I said.

"I'm sorry. I should have spared you that."

In the end, he seemed to lay the blame on Ann. "If only she hadn't kept everything a secret," he said. "We might have helped. Maybe it wouldn't have made any difference, but we'll never know now."

"You don't think this is Ann's fault do you?" I said.

"Of course not," he said sharply. He paused in his walking to look into my face. "I just wish she'd asked for help, that's all."

I was aware of the closeness of his hand. I had to stop myself from catching hold of it. "I think she was just trying to be steady for him," I said. "Her husband was sick, and maybe she really believed he'd get better."

We circled back to the guesthouse, and he paused at the end of the walk. "There's not much point in even talking about it now, is there?" he said. "The boy's gone." He looked back in the direction of the hospital. "And Albert Crenshaw will be dead before the day's over," he said, "if he's not gone already."

I didn't want to cry. He had enough on his hands without having to comfort me.

"He didn't have a chance," he went on, unmistakable anger in his voice now.

"I'm so sorry, Hal." I took his hand, and squeezed it once before I let go.

We went into the guesthouse together, but I didn't feel it was appropriate to go into the parlor with him. I saw the Crenshaws stand up when he came in. They were holding hands. Their stricken faces said they knew what was coming, as I had known, from the moment I heard Betty say "eighty per cent."

22

Dear President Nixon.

I wrote in my best handwriting, but straightforwardly, not allowing myself to fuss over the wording. *I am writing to you about the war, and to tell you what I saw when I visited my son Vincent, who was burned in a helicopter crash in Vietnam.*

It occurred to me that I ought to write to LBJ too, even though he wasn't the one making the decisions any more. I felt a peculiar closeness to LBJ. It wasn't only because of the nights I lay awake listening to the helicopters landing at Fort Sam Houston, wondering if one of them might be his. It was also because I truly felt sorry for him, for the awful responsibility he still had to bear. In a way, his situation was akin to mine — a sad looking back on what it was too late to undo. I never did find out if LBJ had ever visited the burn ward. I suspect they would have protected him from that.

The burn ward is small, I wrote to President Nixon, *but it is crowded with terrible things, so much pain and death. I cannot forget what it is like to see grown men cry.* I told him about Pete Christie and Albert Crenshaw. I told him about the boy I saw in the Cube, the boy so severely burned that he certainly must have died, though his death had somehow been absorbed into all the others and I couldn't actually recall when it happened. I apologized that I didn't even know the boy's name. I cried as I wrote, because I didn't know.

I had to use two pieces of paper, and I worried the letter was probably getting too long. But what were the chances anyway such a letter would really be placed in the president's hands?

I believe it is important that I tell you these things. I wish you would come to the burn ward. I can only tell you that it brings this war home to you, when you see it with your own eyes.

❍

"See you soon, Mom," Vincent said, when I kissed him goodbye. "Oh, and would you give that to Barb?" There was an envelope on the table, with Barbara's name on it, in block print.

"You wrote this?" I said.

"Yup." He reached for a pen imbedded in a thick, padded grip. "Lieutenant Paulson made it for me."

"I'm impressed."

"You should be. Oh — and look in my drawer. Major Trainer left something for you."

It was a stout envelope, something lumpy inside. On the outside, Hal had written *Kitty Duvall*, and underlined it with a firm stroke. I put both envelopes in my pocketbook, and kissed Vincent again.

"Bye, Mom," he said. "See you at home."

As I was leaving the ward, Colonel Anderson stepped around the corner, just the way she did on the first day. "Mrs. Duvall!" She opened her arms and took me in. "You have a safe trip now."

"What will I do without you?"

"You'll do what you did before," she said, letting me go. "And you'll be fine."

I went up to say goodbye on 14A, where the nurses and corpsmen had seen Vincent through the worst. I saw Corporal Jenks and Captain Garcia and Sergeant Berry. *Goodbye, Mrs. Duvall.* They waved to me with exaggerated brightness, but then they turned away, caught again in the undertow of things they had to do at once. I saw Dr. Caruso making his rounds. I managed to catch his eye and wave to him. I looked for Hal, but he wasn't around.

I didn't open the envelope until I got to the airport. Inside I found a picture postcard of the San Fernando Cathedral and something small, twisted up in blue tissue paper. I loosened the paper, and out poured a rosary of silver beads, so small and light I could close my fingers over them and make them disappear. On the back of the postcard Hal had printed his address and phone number, and underneath it one line: *Kitty, this is to replace the one you left at San Fernando. Yours, Hal.*

My flight was delayed, so I bought *The San Antonio Light* at the newsstand and sat reading it by the window overlooking the planes taxiing in and out. All around me young people in uniform were coming and going.

On the front page of *The Light* there was a photograph of President Nixon meeting the troops in a base camp near Saigon. His grinning face was like an apparition on the sea of helmets. Under it was a piece about the victims of Hurricane Camille, but the article in the lower corner caught my eye: *Archbishop visits BAMC.*

It was a short article, with a photograph of the Archbishop leaning down to shake the hand of a patient in a wheelchair. The Archbishop had a kind face. When asked about the morale of the soldiers, he answered, "Wonderful," and went on to say that Vietnam was the last line of defense, and that the young men he visited believed in the American way of life. "They're happy to pay the price," he was quoted as saying. "God's will be done. Not one of them complained."

God's will be done.

But I was thinking of Albert Crenshaw, and of the a boy in the Cube with a tube down his throat, the one who had died — almost all of them on the respirators had died. How many? It was terrible that I couldn't actually sort them out. *Not one of them complained.*

I thought about Mary Kate, her young face twisted with rage: *Mom! It's like you're asleep. How can you let them send Vinnie?*

God's will be done.

But I hadn't been asleep. I'd been alert and doing the work that had always fallen to me — keeping watch over the home, over my children — while the others saw to God's will, whatever that might be, clear on the other side of the world.

I believed that the kindly Archbishop was a holy man, close to God. And yet I felt it had been wrong of him to speak for those wounded boys, to say that they were happy. It occurred to me to throw the newspaper away, but for some reason I didn't. I still had it with me hours later, folded under my arm, when we landed in Baltimore, when Jack and Mary Kate came bursting through the gate to greet me.

On the ground in Baltimore, it seemed to me that Jack was driving too fast, that Mary Kate was talking too fast. As we sped out of the airport, up the Parkway, and through the city toward our little house on Constance Avenue, I struggled to keep up with them in my head.

And then at home, before Jack could even get the suitcase up the front steps, the phone was ringing. Mary Kate ran ahead to get it. "I bet that's Nana!"

My own living room — the faded green chintz slipcovers, the grass summer rug, the wrought-iron floor lamp with the yellowing paper shade — seemed oddly smaller now, as though I'd come home to my childhood.

"She's fine, Nana. Here she is now." Mary Kate was waving me over to the phone.

“Thank God you’re home,” my mother exclaimed on the other end of the line. “You must be exhausted. I had the whole Sodality praying for you.”

I stood numbly in the kitchen, staring at the calendar with the picture of the German shepherd puppies and the words I’d scribbled underneath: *Japan, Brooke Army Medical Center, burn ward.* No one had turned the page to September.

They had put together a cold supper — chicken salad, and rolls from the Woodlea Bakery. The table was set, iced tea prepared. They had even picked mint for me, from the garden out back. Apparently they expected to sit down immediately and eat. And then the doorbell rang — Barbara — and I realized they were expecting her.

All through supper they talked about a party they were going to throw when Vincent came home. I let them go on, waiting for the right moment to remind them Vincent would need his rest. But in the end I held my tongue. Vincent would need friends coming to see him too, and I was already worried those friends might abandon him.

I remembered to give Barbara the letter from Vincent. She opened it right away, moving her dinner plate to the side and laying the single sheet of lined paper before her on the tablecloth. Jack and Mary Kate got up to clear the table, but I watched Barbara read, unable to help myself. As she read, her thick beautiful hair fell forward, hiding her face. And then she held the letter up for me to see. It was just a short note really, printed rather tidily.

“Isn’t he doing great?” she said, putting the letter back in the envelope before I took in more than *Dear Barb* and *miss you.* “I hate to eat and run, but we have this stupid curfew.”

“Run along,” I said. “We don’t want you getting into trouble with the Sisters of Mercy.”

She said goodbye to Jack and Mary Kate at the kitchen door, and I walked her out onto the porch, where I hugged her quickly. “I never said how much it meant to me,” I said, “that you came all the way to Texas to see Vincent.”

“I had to come. I couldn’t leave him alone.” She looked down, suddenly flustered. “Of course you were there with him, but you know what I mean.”

After she was gone, I sat at the table again, where the placemats hadn’t been gathered and the crumbs hadn’t been wiped up. Outside, beyond the curtains puffing out in the breeze, I could hear the children shouting in the alley, the Ackerman's dachshund yapping his little heart out, and the whine of Alma Henderson's hedge shears. I looked around the dining room, imagining what Hal's first impression would be — the African violets under the window and my grandmother's silver teapot on the sideboard, which I hadn't polished since Christmas, and the snapshots of the children, taken on their respective First Communions and graduations, in simple frames from the dime store.

Jack came to say he was going out with friends, and went banging out the back door. Then Mary Kate came to say goodbye too.

"Anything you want before I go, Mom?"

"No. I'm going to get into my nightgown. Tomorrow I'll need an early start on the house."

"What's there to do? Looks clean to me. It's not like Jack's a party animal or anything."

"I know, but I want the fall cleaning done before Vincent comes home."

"It's not fall yet, Mom."

"It's coming."

She laughed. "Well, just so you don't get up on a ladder and start in on the windows tonight." She gave me a fierce hug. "I love you, Mom. I'm glad you're home."

How beautiful she was, with her large brown eyes and flawless skin. Her hair was caught back with two red plastic barrettes in the shape of stars. She was wearing cut-off blue jeans and a T-shirt — no bra underneath apparently, but small as she was, she could almost get away with it.

"I thought about you so much when I was away," I said. "I kept seeing myself as this person who stands around, holding steady, dumb as a post. And all the while you were saying the things that needed to be said."

She sat down beside me. "Give yourself credit," she said. "Look what you managed to do. You flew all the way to Texas to look after Vinnie. You've been to hell and back, and it must have been awfully hard. I'm proud of you. We all are."

"I did what any mother would do."

"I'm not so sure about that." She reached out to my hair, curled a strand around her finger, the way she used to when she was a little girl. "There's a meeting this week at my apartment, Mom. Steve Cavanaugh will be there — my priest friend, remember? — and Sister Cathy. Maybe you'd like to come. It would give you a chance to talk."

"You mean your prayer group?"

She smiled slyly. "I guess you know by now that we do more than pray."

I remembered Easter Sunday, how she had run out of the house in tears and not one of us had got up from the table to go after her, how Bonnie's question had hung sadly in the kitchen the whole time we were washing up the dishes: *What does she want from us, Kitty?*

"If I came to your meeting," I said, "I'd probably sit there like a bump on a log. It takes time for me to think these things through, Mary Kate."

She laid her head on my shoulder. "You'd be a special bump, Mom."

"Did I tell you I saw Will Bishop again?" I said.

"No, but he told me."

"You talked to him?"

"Uh huh. I'm helping him organize some stuff for the Moratorium in October."

How beautiful she was, but I was thinking then of her heart.

I stood on the back porch and watched her walk to the car. Out in the alley, farther down the block, Tooty Cromwell was still working on the innards of his old hotrod — Tooty, who was remembered in the Duvall family for the time he hit Vincent in the face with a snowball and gave him a bloody nose.

"Hi, Tooty!" she called, and gave a beep of the horn. I watched after her until the growl of the little Volkswagen disappeared into the rush of traffic on Belair Road.

Late in the evening Frank called. "So when do you figure Vinnie will come home?" he asked. "I was thinking I'd fly up there to see him." He seemed hesitant, as though he half expected me to say no. "You think that would be a good idea?"

"Of course I do."

"He probably doesn't give a rat's ass about seeing his old man. The last time I saw him he must have been about — What? Thirteen?"

"About that. I'm sure he'll be glad to see you, Frank," I said quickly, "and the main thing is to encourage him to get back to a normal routine. They say that's important."

"Sure," he said. "Like getting right back on the horse, I guess."

"Yes, that's it."

"So look — not to change the subject, but I was wondering — Have you given any thought to making it official? With the divorce, I mean?"

"Is there a reason it has to be official?"

In the pause, I pictured his face — the one smiling crookedly out of the photograph I used to carry in my wallet — and wondered how much it had it changed since I'd actually laid eyes on him.

"I want to get married again," he said. "I could tell you about her, but I don't think you want to hear it."

"Not right now."

"Look, I know you've got a lot on your hands. I'm not asking you to do the paperwork or anything like that. I guess I'm just asking if you're going to fight me on this."

"I'm not going to fight you. What would be the point?"

"Thank you, Kitty. I really mean that. Because I'm finally getting my act together, and Abby — well, she's been looking after me for a while now, and I think I owe it to her."

"Abby."

"Yes. She's a good person, Kitty. You'd like her."

"I would have looked after you, you know."

"I know. I was wrong back then, about a lot of things. And I'm sorry. But that's all water under the bridge, right?"

It was on the tip of my tongue to say yes, all water under the bridge, and I'd forgiven him long ago. But it wasn't really true. All those years, the part of me that might have forgiven had been suspended, like it was frozen in a block of ice.

"Listen," he went on. "I know it's going to cost us for the lawyer and court fees. I'll take care of all that. And if you want an annulment — That doesn't mean squat to me, and Abby's a Lutheran, but if matters to you — "

"No," I said, finding my voice. "No annulment. We'd have to lie. We'd have to say that our marriage vows weren't valid to begin with."

"It's OK," he said, interrupting. "Like I said, I don't care about the Catholic Church. And really, we can talk about all this later. So, I'll let you go now."

"Thank you for buying the plane tickets," I remembered to say. "It meant a lot to me, and to the children too."

"You're welcome. Goodbye now, Kitty."

I pictured him hanging up the phone in a bright kitchen in Florida, turning to a good woman named Abby, both of them relieved to have that step behind them.

The *San Antonio Light* was lying on the kitchen table. It gave me a start to see it there, on top of *The Baltimore Sun*. I put it aside, picked up the *Sun*, and paged through idly, checking the ads for the A & P. At the last minute, out of habit, I ran my eye down the death notices.

The name *Richardson* stopped me. Years before I'd had an obstetrician named Richardson. But this Richardson was Chief Warrant Officer George Richardson, USA, beloved son of James and Marian, and he had died in Vietnam. *In Vietnam* — two words to tell what had happened to him. I searched the previous page, where the longer obituaries generally appeared, but there was no further mention of George Richardson, no photograph.

Only a little paragraph in small type, and yet such crushing weight to it that I was holding my breath as I read. And so many paragraphs just like it appearing all over the country in other newspapers — in Austin for Pete Christie, in Newark for Albert Crenshaw, and I didn't even know in what state Phil Bukowsky would be buried. I'd witnessed these deaths up close, not to mentions the boys in the Cube I never really got to know — Martha Jackson's son, and the Hernandez boy, others whose names I never learned, or had already forgotten because it was just too much to carry.

The funeral Mass for Chief Warrant Officer George Richardson would take place at The Shrine of the Little Flower, only a few miles down the road. I could picture how it would go: the mourners weeping in the pews, the priest moving ceremoniously around the flag-draped coffin, making that solemn clinking noise as he swung the incense high and low.

At the end of the day, it was the stillness of my own room that unsettled me most — the chenille bedspread with the fringe hanging straight and the medallion-pattern perfectly centered, the three baby pictures framed in silver on the dresser, the window shade pulled to the sill, just as I'd left it weeks ago. I raised the shade and opened the window. In came the sad-sweet fragrance of the autumn clematis that weighed down the alley fence every summer and waited to bloom until just around the time the children went back to school. It was almost dark. The light from my window fell on the roof of the old tree house

Frank built. Out in the alley, children were calling to each other on their way home, their voices punctuated by the ringing bounce of a basketball.

I went and got Hal's envelope from my pocketbook, read the card once more, and put it in the drawer. I unwrapped the rosary and settled it on the nightstand, under the lamp.

And then I remembered the letter to President Nixon. I found a stamp for it in the desk, and headed for the mailbox on the corner.

Alma Henderson was still out there in the near dark, sweeping up the hedge clippings from her sidewalk. "You're back," she called. "How's Vincent?"

"He's doing well, thank you," I answered, but kept on moving. "He'll be home in a week or so."

"Well that's good news, if I ever heard it," she called after me.

When I had dropped my letter in the mailbox, I stood a moment and I looked back down Constance Avenue. The face of my own house gazed back at me, utterly changed.

Epilogue

One of my friends at Calvert Park asked me why this story ends where it does. She wanted the rest of the story, how we all went on with our lives. I tried to explain that the rest of the story wasn't the point. But for her sake, and for others like her, I provide the rest below:

After numerous grafts, Vincent recovered, made his way through college and eventually received a degree in occupational therapy. He married Barbara Houck in 1972. They have two children, Hannah and Michael, and one grandchild, little Vincent, a year old now. Barbara still works as a nurse at Mercy Hospital in Baltimore. Vincent isn't one to look back, and rarely talks about the days on the burn ward. Much of it he doesn't remember.

Jack became a pediatric oncologist. He married while still in medical school, but that marriage ended in divorce. He married a second time — a good marriage, though there were no children. He died suddenly of a heart attack in 1996, while jogging alone, one beautiful morning in June. His second wife Elizabeth and I are still close.

Mary Kate married Will Bishop in 1976. She's a published poet and a peace activist. She serves on the council of her parish in San Antonio. She regularly, loudly, calls for the ordination of women in the Catholic Church. She and Will have three children — John, Eric, and Stephanie — all grown now, none married yet. Will is a successful attorney who does a lot of pro bono work for veterans. He plans to run for Congress in 2008.

Ann Bukowsky and I corresponded for a short while, until I lost track of her. Years later, I learned she had died, most likely of the disease they now have a name for — anorexia.

Frank married Abby in 1971, and they had a child right away, a son named Jeremy. They settled in Virginia, where Frank worked for many years in the recycling business. I hear from them at Christmas, a chatty letter Abby prints out on fancy holiday paper. Jeremy teaches at Johns Hopkins here in Baltimore. One day he came to see me, a really delightful visit. He said his father had suggested he come.

Hal left the Army in 1970 and followed me to Baltimore. We married in 1973, sold the house on Constance Avenue, and moved to West Virginia, where he served as pastor for a small church near Elkins. We had many happy years in West Virginia. When he retired, we returned to Baltimore to be close to the children. His death last year was unexpected, for he'd always been so healthy and strong. And yet I have to say a person couldn't ask for a more peaceful death than his, in his sleep.

I now go to Mass every Sunday with Vincent and his family at a Catholic Church downtown — St. Vincent's, just a coincidence in the name. After all those years of banishment because of my marriage to Hal, one day I saw the light: It was foolishness to hang back from the sacraments I loved, like a child unjustly punished, still sulking over it.

On June 4, 2006, my great-grandchild Vincent was baptized, and as I was coming back from Communion, I glanced at my son Vincent, the proud grandfather in the front pew. He gave me a big smile and an outrageous thumbs-up.

That moment might have been a good place to end this story. But I bring it full circle now, and end instead on a moment after, when the priest stepped into the pulpit and asked us to pray — another soldier killed, this time in Vincent's own parish.

Let us not forget the others, I prayed — am still praying, even as I write. *Let us not forget the soldiers in hospitals, far from their mothers and home.*

About the Author

Madeleine Mysko is a registered nurse who served as a lieutenant in the Army Nurse Corps at Brooke Army Medical Center during the Vietnam War. Since then, her creative energies have been devoted to writing. She holds a master's degree in English Literature from The George Washington University and a master's degree from the Writing Seminars of The Johns Hopkins University. Her work — both poetry and prose — has been published widely in journals, including *American Journal of Nursing, The Baltimore Sun, Bellevue Literary, The Christian Century, The Hudson Review, Maryland Poetry Review, River Styx*, and *Shenandoah*. Among her awards are two individual artist grants from the Maryland State Arts Council, a Howard Nemerov Sonnet Award, and a Baltimore City Artscape Prize. She teaches creative writing in the Advanced Academic Programs of The Johns Hopkins University, and lives with her husband in Towson, Maryland.

Photo by Miriam Berkley

Printed in the United States
94623LV00001B/12/A

9 781891 386787